Books by Robert B. Parker

THE GODWULF MANUSCRIPT
GOD SAVE THE CHILD
MORTAL STAKES
PROMISED LAND

THREE WEEKS IN SPRING
(with Joan Parker)

THE JUDAS GOAT
WILDERNESS
LOOKING FOR RACHEL WALLACE
EARLY AUTUMN
A SAVAGE PLACE
CEREMONY
THE WIDENING GYRE
LOVE AND GLORY
VALEDICTION

VALEDICTION

Robert B. Parker

A DELL/SEYMOUR LAWRENCE BOOK

A SEYMOUR LAWRENCE BOOK
Published by
Dell Publishing Co., Inc.
1 Dag Hammarskjold Plaza
New York, New York 10017

Dell ® TM 681510, Dell Publishing Co., Inc.

ISBN: 0-440-19247-1

Reprinted by arrangement with Delacorte Press/Seymour
Lawrence
Printed in the United States of America

First Dell printing—April 1985

For Joan, like gold to airy thinness beat

Dull sublunary lovers' love
   (Whose soul is sense) cannot admit
Absence, because it doth remove
   Those things which elemented it.

John Donne,
A Valediction: Forbidding Mourning

VALEDICTION

CHAPTER 1

There were at least three kinds of cops in Harvard Yard: a scattering of Cambridge cops, gray-haired mostly, with faces out of County Mayo; portly old men in brown uniforms and no sidearms who guarded the gates; and squadrons of Harvard University police who wore tailored blue uniforms and expensive black gun belts, and looked like graduates of the Los Angeles Police Academy. It was Harvard commencement, and if the WASPs began to run amok, Harvard was ready. I was ready too. I had a Smith & Wesson Chief's Special clipped onto my belt just back of my right pants pocket where the butt caused only a modest break in the line of my silk tweed jacket. The jacket was off-white with a faint blue weave and came from Brooks Brothers. It wasn't my favorite, but the choices are not wide in off-the-rack size 48's.

On a folding chair among many many folding chairs set up on the broad lawn between Widener Library and Memorial Church, Susan Silverman sat in a black gown and a funny-looking mortarboard and waited for the formal award of her Ph.D. in clinical psychology. I was there to watch and although I had a seating ticket I found myself getting restless very early and began to wander around the yard and look at the preparations for postcommencement festivities when graduates are congratulated and classes are reunited and funds are raised.

All about me the subdued and confident honk of affluent Yankee voices, male and female, murmured a steady counterpoint to the Latin dissertation being delivered from the commencement platform and redelivered over speakers throughout the area. It had been the excitement of the Latin address that had initially got me up and walking around and eyeing the barrels of free beer hooked to the taps, ready to be broached when the graduates were official.

The Latin address gave way to an English

disquisition on the Legacy of Confusion, which in turn gave way to an English address on the Moral Life. On the steps of Boylston Hall a bunch of men in top hats and tails were having their pictures taken with a bunch of women in white dresses and red sashes. I went into the basement of Boylston Hall to use the men's room. No one else was there. Maybe one didn't do that at a Harvard commencement. Maybe Harvard people didn't do that at all.

Finally it was over and Susan met me by the beer table, pushing her way past a procession from Quincy House that was being led out by a guy blowing bagpipes.

"How do you like it so far," she said.

I kissed her on the mouth. "I don't know that I've ever screwed a doctor," I said.

She nodded. "Yes, I knew you'd have just the right thing ready to say."

Even in her cap and gown Susan looked like a sunrise, extravagant and full of promise. Wherever she went things seemed, as they always did, to organize around her.

She smiled at me. "Shall we have some of the revolting chicken salad?"

"Your graduation," I said.

We had the chicken salad and a couple of free beers and watched everything and spoke very little. Susan was excited. I could see it in her face. She was looking at everything and barely eating. I looked mostly at her, as I always did, trying somehow to encompass the density and elegance of her. *Never enough,* I thought. *It's like air, you never tire of breathing it.*

"Did you like the ceremony?" Susan said.

I nodded. "The Latin dissertation made my blood race."

"But it really is wonderful, don't you think?"

I shrugged.

"I know it's silly, but it's very exciting. It's full of tradition and it makes me feel like a real part of something. It's what a graduation ought to be."

"And you are now a doctor. Dr. Silverman. You like that?"

She nodded.

Around the yard, hanging from old brick buildings, were signs designating class years —1957, 1976—and old grads were gathering under those banners to talk about how fast they could run when they were young, and get zonkered on bloody Marys and vodka martinis in clear plastic cups.

"You going back to D.C.?" I asked it casually, glancing around at the Radcliffe graduates. But my stomach wasn't casual when I

16

said it. My stomach was clenched tight and full of dread.

Susan shook her head a little vaguely, one of those little head gestures she made that meant neither yes nor no.

"Chicken salad really isn't very good, is it?" she said.

"No, it's awful," I said. "But the servings are small."

CHAPTER 2

At six o'clock we were sitting at the counter in my kitchen sharing a victory bottle of Cuvée Dom Pérignon, 1971.

"Veritas," I said to Susan. She smiled and we drank. My kitchen window was open and the breeze that blew off the Charles River basin moved a few of the outer curls on Susan's dark hair. It had been sunny all day, but now it was ominous-looking outside with dark clouds, and the breeze was chilly.

Between us on a large plate there was French bread and wheat crackers and goat cheese, milk-white with a dark outer coating, and some nectarines and a bunch of pale green seedless grapes.

Susan said, "I've taken a job in San Francisco."

I put the glass down on the counter. I could feel myself begin to shrink inward.

"I'm leaving tonight," she said. "I had planned to stay the night with you and tell you in the morning, but I can't. I can't not tell you."

"How long," I said.

"I don't know. I've thought about it for a long time. All the last year in Washington when I was doing my internship."

It began to rain outside my kitchen window. The rain coming straight down from the darkened sky, quietly, with a soft hiss.

"I have to be alone," Susan said.

"For how long?"

"I don't know. You can't ask me, because I really don't."

"I'll visit you."

"Not right away. I have to be by myself. For a while anyway, I don't want you to know my address."

Bubbles continued to drift up from the bottom of the champagne glass, spaced more as the champagne flattened, coming sparsely and with leisure. Neither of us drank.

"You have a place to stay out there?"

"Yes. I've arranged that already."

19

Her hair stirred again. The wind was cold now, and damp from the rain that moved steadily downward through it. One lightning flash flared a moment at the window and then, an appreciable time later, the thunder rolled in behind it.

"I called Paul," Susan said. "He'll be here in the morning. I didn't want you to be alone."

I nodded. The curtains at the kitchen window moved in the cold breeze. Susan stood up. I stood with her.

"I'm going to go now," she said.

I nodded.

She put her arms around me and said, "I do love you."

"I love you."

She squeezed me and put her cheek against mine. Then she stepped away and turned and walked toward the door.

"I'll call you," she said, "when I get to San Francisco."

"Yes."

She opened the door and looked back at me.

"Are you all right," she said.

I shook my head.

"Paul will come tomorrow," she said. "I'll call you soon."

Then she went out and closed the door and I was alone with my soul dwindled to icy stillness at the densely compacted center of myself.

CHAPTER 3

When Paul Giacomin arrived I was still sitting at the counter. The champagne bottle was full of flat champagne and the two glasses, half drunk, were beside it. I was drinking coffee. Outside, the rain fell with undeviating purpose.

Paul put his suitcase down and came over. "How are you," he said.

I shook my head.

"Susan gone?" he said.

I nodded. "Last night," I said.

He started the burner under the hot water. "You sleep?" he said.

"No."

"You understand this?" Paul said. The

water heated quickly because I had just used some. He poured the boiling water into a cup and added a spoonful of coffee, and stirred. He always made coffee that way.

"Yes," I said. I stood and went and looked out the window in the living room. It was raining out there too.

"I'm willing to listen if you want to talk about it," Paul said. "Or I'm willing to shut up if you want to do that."

"Talking may be overrated," I said.

"Maybe," Paul said. "But you'll think about it. Whether or not you talk is just whether or not you share what you're thinking."

"Smartass college kid," I said.

The morning was a dark background on Marlborough Street, people going to work carried colorful striped umbrellas, students going to summer school wore blue and green and yellow slickers, the flowers in the small yards glistened in the rain and the street itself gleamed wetly. The traffic was mostly cabs and the cabs were mostly yellow.

"When she went to Washington," I said, "and did her predoctoral internship she got a taste of being a full person, nobody's wife, nobody's girlfriend, nobody's employee, but a full professional person whose worth was in her knowledge and her insight and her compassion."

Paul sipped his coffee. I leaned my head against the window and watched the street glisten.

"She couldn't be that with you?" Paul said.

"I think she's trying to find out what she can be," I said. "I have . . . I have a view of the world that is pretty fully formed . . . and I cling to that view pretty hard. It doesn't leave Susan too much room. Or you."

"I don't think Susan disagrees with too much of what you hold to be self-evident," Paul said.

I shrugged.

"On the other hand, perhaps she'd like to arrive at those truths herself."

"Yes," I said. "Or maybe think her own thoughts and not have to compare them with mine."

Paul came and stood beside me and looked down at Marlborough Street with me.

"You wondering if maybe you've been a little too rigid?" Paul said.

"I'm considering the possibility that there are ways to be a good person that I hadn't thought of," I said.

"Might help loosen things up for you," Paul said. "It must always have been hard being you."

"Not as hard as this," I said.

"I know."

The wind had strengthened coming off the river and the flower petals began to litter the sidewalk, limp and wet.

"I won't quit on this," I said.

"Pressing her will make it worse," Paul said.

"I know."

"So what will you do?"

"For now I'll wait."

"Then what?"

"I don't know."

Paul nodded. "Hard," he said. "Hard as hell not to know."

We were quiet. There wasn't anything to say. Below me some of the wet flower petals on the sidewalk washed into the gutter. And the rain kept coming.

CHAPTER 4

Henry Cimoli had a full range of Nautilus
equipment installed at the Harbor Health
Club. The whole place was getting out of
hand. There were women in there now as
well as men. There was a lounge where you
could sit around in a velour sweat suit and
drink carrot juice, there had been complaints
that the speed bag in the boxing room made
too much noise, and some of the people working on the Nautilus wore Lacoste shirts. Hawk
had told Henry that if anyone came in to work
out wearing Top-Siders that he, Hawk, would
demand a refund on his membership.

"Hawk," Henry said, "you come here free."

"Fucking place is full of guys in tennis shorts," Hawk said.

"Hell, you even get the tanning booth free," Henry said.

Hawk looked at him. "Wimp city," he said, and walked away.

"He just don't understand upscale," Henry said.

A club member stopped beside us to sign in. He was wearing a dark blue sweatband on his head and dark blue wristbands and a raspberry-colored Lacoste shirt and white tennis shorts and knee socks with red and blue stripes around the top and Fred Perry tennis shoes. There was a Sony Walkman at his waist and fluffy red earphones over the sweatband. He smelled of Brut.

I looked at Henry. "Wimp city," I said, and went after Hawk.

Hawk worked out in a pair of old boxing shorts and high boxer's shoes and no shirt. When I joined him he was doing chest presses on the machine. He had the pin in at maximum weight and was doing the exercises with no visible effort except for the glistening film of sweat. With the gym lights glaring down on him the black skin on his torso and shaved head gleamed like the wet asphalt had the morning Susan left. People watched him covertly as the muscles in his arms and chest bunched and relaxed.

I did some curls. It was hard to do what until recently I had done easily.

When I got through Hawk was off the bench press machine and we swapped places.

In the boxing room I never did get a good rhythm on the speed bag and there was no bite in my punches on the heavy bag. Hawk made it dance, but I just bludgeoned it. We took some steam and then showered. We were the only ones in the shower room.

"Something wrong with you," Hawk said. It wasn't a question.

"You just noticed?" I said.

"Besides being a honkie and a preppie and a fucking bleeding heart. Something wrong with you."

"Susan moved to San Francisco," I said.

Hawk let the hot water run over him and the lathered soap slid away.

"Get dressed," Hawk said. "I buy you a drink."

We walked across Atlantic Avenue to the Market and sat at the bar in J. J. Donovan's Tavern. I had Irish whiskey on the rocks.

"You still drinking that stuff," Hawk said.

"True to my heritage," I said.

"What do I drink?"

"Rum."

Hawk ordered Mount Gay rum on the rocks. "Rum, religion, and slaves," he said.

"Cradle of liberty."

The drinks came. We had a taste.

"What she doing in San Francisco," Hawk said.

"Job."

"You going to visit?"

"I don't know her address."

We drank some more.

"She going to tell you where she lives?" Hawk said.

"Maybe in a while."

"Want me to find her?" he said.

"No. She's got the right to be private."

"She got somebody out there?" Hawk said.

"I don't know."

"If she got somebody, I can kill him," Hawk said.

I shook my head again. "She's got a right to somebody else," I said. Hawk gestured another round at the bartender.

"You too," Hawk said.

"I don't want anyone else."

"Thought you wouldn't."

The thing I like about Irish whiskey is that the more you drink the smoother it goes down. Of course that's probably true of antifreeze as well, but illusion is nearly all we have. The bar was half empty. Two young

29

women sat at the bar near the door and kept an eye out. A young couple played Space Invaders behind us in the corner.

One of the young women at the door was looking at Hawk. There was interest in her look, and fear.

"Take some balance," Hawk said. It was as if he were thinking out loud. "Be like carrying a glass of water filled right to the top and not spilling any. Be a bitch."

"Yes," I said.

"This is something you can't fix," Hawk said. "You got to trust her to do it."

"It's my life, in some sense or other."

Hawk nodded. "I'd trust Susan with mine," he said.

I looked at Hawk's peaceful, deadly face. Obsidian skin tight over intricate muscle and prominent bone.

"Yes," I said. "I would too."

CHAPTER 5

Paul was with me for the summer. He had a job with a small company in Boston called the Tommy Banks Dancers. The pay was negligible, but it was a chance to perform and Tommy Banks was, Paul said, legitimate.

"Performance is different," Paul said. "You can take classes all your life, and rehearse forever, but you make more progress in one performance than you do in a year of lessons."

We were having dinner, in my kitchen.

"Sure," I said. "Performance is the actual thing. The other stuff is getting ready."

Supper was cold poached salmon fillets with dill mayonnaise, and boiled new potatoes and peapods. Paul got up to get a second

31

bottle of Rolling Rock Extra Pale from the refrigerator. He held it up at me, I shook my head. He opened it and sat back down.

"You feel like working?" he said.

"Have to eventually," I said.

"One of the dancers in the company has disappeared."

"Cops been notified?"

Paul shook his head. "Tommy doesn't want them. It's his girlfriend."

"Why no cops?"

"I don't know. It's a little strange. But I told Tommy I'd ask you. Are you ready to do something? I don't want you to do it unless you're ready."

"Better than hanging around watching *Family Feud,*" I said.

Paul drank some beer from the bottle. "I knew you'd be enthusiastic," he said.

The phone rang. I answered on the first ring. Susan's voice said, "Hello."

It was difficult to get air in. I said, "How are you?"

Paul looked at me and then got up and walked to the living room and turned on the television.

"Good," Susan said. "I'm good. How are you?"

"Functional," I said. "Sort of."

"Paul still there?"

32

"Yes, He'll be here all summer."

"Are you working?"

"I haven't. But Paul's asked me to do something. And I said I would. I'm having a little trouble with my energy levels."

"Yes," Susan said.

"You got a nice apartment?" I said.

"Yes. It's small. But it's modern. I'm subletting it for a couple of months. You want my telephone number?"

"Yes," I said.

She gave it. "Are you going to be all right?" she said.

"Depends," I said. "Depends on your definition of all right. And it depends on how our relationship works out."

"When I left," Susan said, "it was not my intention to end the relationship. I have done what I wanted to do. I have gotten to be alone. Now I've just got to experience being alone for a while and see where it leads."

As there often is on coast-to-coast calls, there were echoes of my voice and hers, and a kind of transmission delay so that our voices tended to overlap. The call was like air to a diver, and the transmission distortions were like kinks in the air hose.

Susan said, "I'm in such a kind of tumbling series of changes that I hate to speak in absolutes. But I would be much less happy if you weren't in some sense part of my life."

"Okay," I said.

"Is this phone driving you crazy too?" she said.

"I get an echo," I said.

"Me too. Not a good time for a bad transmission."

"No," I said. "When my energy levels get up high enough I may go down to AT&T and bust up some executive's bridgework."

"Okay," she said. "I'm going to hang up now. I've been charging around since I got here, and I'm exhausted and I've been so worried about you I can't breathe."

"I'm okay," I said. "I'm much better now that I've talked to you."

"I'll talk to you soon," Susan said.

"I love you," I said.

"Yes," Susan said. And hung up.

Paul was watching the Muppets on Channel Nine. I poured some Irish whiskey into a glass and went in and sat down and sipped the whiskey and told him about Susan's conversation.

"That's encouraging," he said.

"Yes."

On the tube Floyd was singing a duet with Pearl Bailey.

"You ought to date," Paul said.

"How about I get a Qiana shirt and some gold chains and tight pants with no pockets . . ."

"And a bulger," Paul said.

"Yeah," I said, "and shoes with Cuban heels, and maybe have my hair styled and blow-dried."

"On the other hand," Paul said, "maybe you hadn't ought to date."

CHAPTER 6

I watched the Tommy Banks Dancers go through a series of tap steps. Paul was one, not featured but clearly a necessary member. The room was small and hot and shabby, on a second floor on Huntington Avenue over a liquor store that advertised 10,000 cases of ice-cold beer. The dancers glistened with sweat. Paul rehearsed in a pair of gray sweat pants held up by a blue and red belt and a red T-shirt that said Puma on the front. The sleeves had been cut off and the neck cut out so that it was little more than a sleeveless undershirt.

Now that I knew Susan's phone number, I could easily find her address. On the other hand, if she wanted me to know her address, she'd tell me.

The dancers took a break in the rehearsal and Tommy Banks came over to meet me. Paul came with him. Banks wore a pair of black knit dance pants and a net polo shirt cut off the way defensive backs on Southern college football teams cut them off so that the stomach is bare. He was shorter than Paul and stocky for a dancer and considerably older than Paul, nearly forty, probably. His hair was cut short and receded from his forehead.

"Mr. Spenser," he said. "Nice of you to come over."

We shook hands. Whatever his age and height, he was in shape. Fine little muscle patterns moved in Banks's flat stomach. We got some coffee from an automatic drip coffeemaker on a card table in one corner of the room next to the record player. The dancers lounged around smoking and drinking coffee and stretching.

"How much has Paul filled you in," Banks said.

"Just that one of your dancers is missing and you want me to find her."

"Well"—Banks made a tight half smile—"that's the essence of it, isn't it."

I nodded.

"She's more than missing," Banks said. "She's been taken."

Paul looked startled. I nodded again.

"She's been taken by the Bullies."

Paul looked more startled. "The religious group?" I said.

"Yes," Banks said. "The Reorganized Church of the Redemption. You know about it, I assume."

"I know that it exists, that its leader, pope, chief wizard, whatever they call him, is a guy named Bullard Winston who believes in the church militant."

"Yes," Banks said. "They've taken Sherry."

"By force?"

"Yes."

"You didn't tell me that," I said to Paul.

"I didn't know it," Paul said.

"They broke in," Banks said, "five of them, three men, two women, in berets and fatigue clothes. They had automatic weapons. One of them hit me with the butt of the weapon and knocked me down. I was half conscious. They grabbed Sherry, bound her, and took her away. I was able to get to the door in time to see them put her into the trunk of a car and drive away. Then I passed out."

"And you didn't call the cops," I said.

Banks shook his head. "I—I woke up and didn't know what to do and . . . I just walked around all night and came in the next day and said Sherry was missing."

"Why no cops?"

"I didn't want this turned into a media circus like Patty Hearst."

I didn't say anything. Paul was quiet, standing a little to the side.

"And . . . I didn't . . . you know how Patty Hearst's fiancé was treated in the press."

I nodded.

"I was ashamed," he said. "I was ashamed that they were able to take her away from me and I didn't stop them."

"Five people with automatic weapons," I said. "Hard to stop."

"I could have died trying."

"I'm not sure we'd be better off," I said.

Banks shook his head as if he were trying to shake something off. "Well, anyway. The company has chipped in and I have a bit of money, and we wish to hire you to find her."

"Okay," I said. "I'll need her picture."

Banks went to get it. I looked at Paul. Paul shrugged. Banks came back with a manila folder in which was a publicity picture of a young woman and a typed résumé, and a handwritten description on white paper lined with blue. I looked at it. Her name was Sherry Spellman and she was twenty years old.

"She have much contact with the Bullies before," I said.

"Oh, hell," Banks said, "she had a little, ah, flirtation I suppose you'd say, while she was in college, but . . ." He shook his head and made a dismissing shrug. I looked back down at her résumé. She'd gone one year to Bard College, leaving two years ago. She'd been with Banks a year.

"No calls," I said, "no ransom notes?"

Banks shook his head.

"Why did they take her?" I said.

"To make her one of them," Banks said. "We can't let them do that."

"No," I said. "I guess we can't."

CHAPTER 7

I called Martin Quirk at police headquarters and got the name of a priest who consulted to the department on oddball cults and religions.

"Named Keneally," Quirk said. "Professor of Comparative Religion at B.C. Use my name."

It had been a while since I'd been in my office. It was stuffy, and the warm city air coming through the open windows wasn't doing much to freshen it up. I looked out the window. The dark-haired art director in the ad agency across the street was conferring over her board with two colleagues. Too busy to look in my window. Probably resigning.

Probably going to take a job in Miami doing bilingual dope ads.

I called up Wayne Cosgrove at the *Globe*.

"Who's your dance critic," I said.

"Nancy Quentin," he said.

"Would you speak to her about me and tell her I'll call her and invite her to lunch."

"You seen Nancy?" Wayne said.

"Business," I said. "I need some dance information."

"Okay. Her extension is 2616. Call her in a half-hour or so. I'll have talked with her by then."

"Unless she's out on assignment," I said.

"Assignment? It's ten thirty in the morning. How many fucking dance recitals you see at ten thirty in the morning?"

"Okay," I said. "I'll call her at eleven."

I hung up and looked out my window some more. It was sunny. The art director and her colleagues had moved away from her board and out of sight somewhere back in the office across the street.

At eleven I called Nancy Quentin.

"A detective," she said. "Very exciting for us arts-and-leisure types."

"I imagine so," I said. "Would you have lunch with me at the Ritz Café?"

"Today?"

"Yes."

"I'll be there in an hour. How will I recognize you?"

"I'll be in the lobby by the café looking out of place," I said.

"See you there," she said, and hung up.

I walked down Berkeley Street to my apartment on Marlborough and put on a tie and my blue blazer with the tattersall lining, and strolled up Arlington to the Ritz. They'd put up a second tower beside the hotel and filled it with condominium apartments that sold for a lot. The new building blended pretty well with the original. It didn't improve anything but it didn't look like a bad case of mange either. When I turned in through the revolving doors it was 11:40. Time for a drink.

I sat at the bar and had an Irish whiskey on the rocks with a twist and ate some peanuts and sipped the drink. I looked at my watch. Eleven fifty. Almost nine o'clock in San Francisco. At 11:55 I finished the drink and walked out into the lobby. A big hard-looking guy with gray hair and a large stomach was going up the curving rose-carpeted stairway toward the dining room. He paused on the stairs and looked at me and nodded.

"Callahan," I said. "Still got that roll of dimes?"

He smiled and nodded. "Business or pleasure?" he said to me.

"Lunch with a client," I said. "Nothing to do with the house."

Callahan nodded again, pleasantly. "Enjoy," he said.

I went and stood outside the café, near the desk, and waited. At ten past noon a woman about the size of the Gadsden Purchase came up to me and said, "Mr. Spenser."

I said yes and she said she was Nancy Quentin and I said, "Shall we to the café?" and in we went.

The café at the Ritz would be the coffee shop in another hotel, but here it really was a café. The food was good, the service elegant, the menu brief but interesting. It was a ground-floor room and there were windows to sit by. In the evening a young woman in a gown played the harp.

The waiter asked if we'd like a cocktail. Nancy had Campari and soda. I had another Irish whiskey.

Nancy looked over at me. "You're right," she said. "You do look out of place."

"And I'm wearing a Brooks Brothers tie too."

"It's not enough," she said.

"I went to the Harvard commencement this year."

"That would help," she said. "But only if

44

you were still wearing your little Harvard commencement badge."

"Yeah. I thought about it but was afraid I'd get caught. People would start asking me smart questions and they'd find out I'd never been."

"Yes," she said. "That is a danger."

She was a very large-boned, tall woman, and she had managed to keep her weight up. She was probably fifty-five and wore a loose-fitting dress with a small gray print in it, and a large straw hat. For her to find a loose-fitting dress was something of a triumph, I thought. She wore a lot of makeup, badly applied. There was lipstick on her teeth. If she'd been a dancer, it must have been in *Fantasia*.

"At the commencement, people were asking really tough ones," I said. "Who's your broker? Where can I get a deal on Volvo station wagons, that kind of stuff. I felt really humble."

She laughed. "I went to Wellesley," she said. "I could have answered those questions easily."

"And now you write for the *Globe?* My God."

"Yes, plucky of me, I think."

The waiter took our order. I had lobster salad. Nancy had the minute steak. We had another round of drinks as well.

"What can you tell me about a dancer named Tommy Banks," I said.

"Ah-ha," Nancy said, "enough with the small talk."

"Yes," I said, "off with the clothes."

She smiled again. "Tommy Banks," she said. Outside our window, on Newbury Street, a man and woman were walking an Afghan hound. The woman's arm was through the man's. He was much taller than she was and occasionally she banged her head against his upper arm as they walked, then looked up at him and laughed about something. Maybe the dog. It's hard not to laugh at an Afghan hound.

"Tommy Banks," Nancy said. "If commitment were all it took, he'd have been Nureyev, or Fred Astaire."

"Talent?"

"Are you a baseball fan, Spenser?"

"Yes."

"His desire is Cooperstown. His talent is Pawtucket."

I nodded.

"He was in New York for a while, studied with Cunningham, danced as a chorus boy with some actress in a one-woman show, Debbie Reynolds, I think—you know, the star and four dancers who serve as context. He formed a tap company of his own, and got some grant

46

money and did a few colleges and Summer thing kinds of appearances, Citicorp Center at noon, that kind of stuff; and then he packed it in and came back to Boston. I believe he felt New York commercialism was stifling. Here he has a school, and a company that instructs at the school and is drawn from it and he works at expanding the tap-dance form."

"Is he being successful?"

She smiled. The waiter brought my lobster salad and Nancy's steak. Susan would have had only an appetizer. Probably smoked salmon. Maybe one glass of white wine, which she wouldn't finish. Nancy ordered a beer. I joined her.

"Successful?" Nancy said. "No, not very. I can applaud his attempt to enlarge the narrative possibilities of tap, but his actual innovations are less successful than the conception, if you follow what I'm saying. Are you familiar with dance?"

"A little," I said. "I have a friend who dances."

"In some ways Tommy would be best in an academic setting where his experiments wouldn't have to be self-supporting. His imagination is limited."

"Do you know about him as a person?"

"Not very much. We've met but I don't know him well. I know he's very driven by an ambition that overleaps his skills. He is, I believe, a very tough disciplinarian with his dancers, and people in the business don't like him very much."

"How about one of his dancers, Sherry Spellman?"

Nancy shook her head. "No. I don't know her."

I had finished my lobster salad and my beer. Three whiskies and a beer at midday and I was feeling mushy. Nancy ate the last of her steak. "Why are you interested in all this?" she said.

"Off the record?" I'd always wanted to say that to a reporter.

"Deep background," Nancy said.

"Sherry's missing. Banks claims she was kidnapped by the Reorganized Church of the Redemption."

Nancy raised her eyebrows. "The Bullies kidnapped her?"

"That's what Banks said."

"You sound skeptical," she said.

"Not really skeptical, it's a deep-seated habit I've developed from spending the last twenty years talking with people who speak with forked tongue."

"Cynical," she said.

"More than that. The story doesn't make a lot of sense. First of all, it sounds just like the

48

Hearst kidnapping, and second, Banks never called the cops. Says he doesn't want a media circus like the Hearst case."

"That may be the definition of ego," Nancy said. "Imagining yourself worthy of a media circus. The Hearsts maybe, but Tommy Banks?"

"I know. He also said he was ashamed that he hadn't died trying to save her."

She shrugged. "More convincing. I believe he has some kind of belt in karate. But . . ." Nancy shrugged and widened her eyes.

"Five people with automatic weapons—doesn't make much difference what kind of belt you have."

"I would think not," Nancy said.

The waiter took our dessert order. Nancy had apple pie and cheese. I had black coffee.

"Why would they take her," Nancy said.

"Banks says they want to make her one of them."

"Aggressive proselytizing," Nancy said. "But why her, why not me, or you? You look like you might be hard, but you see what I'm asking."

"Banks said she'd been involved before. 'A brief flirtation when she was in college,' he said."

"And once a Bullie, always a Bullie?"

"I don't know. That's my next stop. I'm consulting a specialist on fruitcakes."

"Fruitcakes? How unsympathetic a view of religion," Nancy said. There was a small swallow of beer left in my glass. I drank it.

"Malt does more than Milton can," I said, "to justify God's ways to man."

CHAPTER 8

The priest was an arrogant one, full of his own knowledge and the pleasures of his impending salvation. But he knew a lot about the Reorganized Church of the Redemption and if I had to suffer a certain amount of foolishness to get the information, I could smile and smile and be agnostic.

"The Bullies," he said, "are a macho subspecies of Christianity. They believe in the concept of Christian soldiers and worship the Christ who scourged the moneylenders from the temple, not He who suffered His own crucifixion."

I smiled and nodded. We were in Father Keneally's office at B.C., a big corner room in one of the handsome graystone buildings on the Quadrangle. On the walls there were pictures of Keneally with Cardinal Cushing, with a couple of former governors, and standing with an arm around the shoulders of a football player named Fred Smerlas. Smerlas was enormous and Keneally was not and the gesture looked strained. The opposite wall was covered with books on shelves and as Keneally talked I had no reason to doubt that he'd read them all.

"Would they kidnap somebody?"

Keneally raised his eyebrows. He was small and neat with an expensive black summer priest suit, and pink healthy-looking skin and crisp white hair cut short. He smelled of bay rum and his nails appeared to have been manicured. A decanter of wine, maybe port, stood on the windowsill and the afternoon sun slanting through it made a purple gleam on the beige Oriental rug that covered the office floor.

"Kidnapping is not part of most Christian rituals," he said.

I wanted to sigh. It was the kind of answer he'd give.

"Neither was the rack and the strappado, as far as I know," I said.

The priest steepled his hands and placed them against his lower lip and nodded, smiling slightly. "You might think of these people as a kind of Christian version of the Jewish Defense League. They are activist. They might use force to achieve the goals of the religion."

"Is it really a religion," I said.

"Are you asking me to define religion, Spenser? In one sense a religion is a religion if it says it is a religion. The Bullies believe in a supreme being and a system of conduct derived from that supreme being's teachings and precepts."

Sigh.

"Religious belief is rather like love," Keneally said. "It can manifest itself in various experiential forms."

"Is Bullard Winston a genuine religious leader?" I said. "Or is he a charlatan."

"Power corrupts, Spenser. Absolute power corrupts absolutely. Winston certainly appeared sincere at the outset, but now I can't be sure. There was some talk of drug use once, but nothing more than ecumenical gossip. Few men are immune to the temptations that reside in absolute authority. Those who resist most successfully are perhaps the recipients of divine aid."

Keneally leaned back in his swivel chair and crossed his ankles on the desktop. A fortunate recipient of divine aid. His black oxfords gleamed with polish.

"How does the church feel about Winston's chances for divine aid?"

"There is, in my view, and it reflects the best thinking currently in the church, little justification for the Bullies' militancy in doctrinal sources, in patristic writing, or in scripture."

"How big," I said.

"Membership? Perhaps ten thousand nationwide. The founding church is here, in Middleton, and there are mission churches in a number of cities across the country and abroad—somewhere in the Middle East and Southeast Asia, I've heard. It seems to have a good funding base, and seems to be well managed."

"You have an address for the church headquarters?"

"No, but it is in Middleton and should be listed in the phone book."

"Okay," I said. "I'll go visit them. Any summation you'd care to give me before I go?"

"I don't know how much reason you have to be wary of these people," Keneally said, "but I have none. As far as I know the church leaders and membership are sincere, if doctrinally unsophisticated. The Bullies pose no threat to the established church or, as far as I know, to the established order. Its membership is probably disenchanted with more orthodox worship, and like so many other fringe religions, the Bullies provide a complete life, albeit a limited one. It is communal, rather rigidly ruled, and vigorously organized by a single purpose. Certain kinds of people find it a very attractive alternative to lives that have been chaotic or aimless."

"The Bullies are not the only source for that kind of satisfaction," I said.

"Indeed not." Keneally smiled. "Many in my calling are drawn by something not dissimilar. But the Bullies also, of course, represent an antiestablishment, and—for lack of a better word—revolutionary, option. The established churches are just that, established, and would thus be less inviting to a certain kind of person."

"A life with mission and without uncertainty," I said, "with some revolutionary zeal for frosting."

Keneally nodded. "One could do worse," he said.

"One often does," I said.

CHAPTER 9

The founding church of the Reorganized Church of the Redemption was on the former site of an animal park and theme village off Route 114 in Middleton. There were about fifteen acres with a green, and a plain white church at one end. Several bungalows lined each side of the green and behind them some small outbuildings, and then gardens. The whole thing looked like a cut-rate version of Old Sturbridge Village.

I pulled in onto the gravel drive that circled the green and drove up and parked beside the church. It looked like any New England village church. In the gardens behind the bungalows a number of people were working.

I walked up the front steps of the church and into the foyer. A sign said OFFICE, and an arrow pointed left. I went left. There was a set of stairs and another arrow. I followed the arrow down and in the basement of the church found a collection of office cubicles separated by frosted glass partitions. There was air-conditioning and fluorescent light and the sound of typewriters. A young woman at the reception desk said, "May I help you."

She had a frizzy perm and some makeup. She wore a white blouse with a round collar and an olive skirt.

"Is there someone who normally talks to people with questions," I said.

"Questions about the church, sir?"

"Yes."

"Mr. Owens is our director of community relations," she said.

"May I speak with him," I said.

"Certainly, sir. Would you have a seat. I'll see if Mr. Owens is free."

I sat and she stood, and walked down the corridor. She was wearing high-heeled shoes with no backs and her tan legs were bare. *Not bad hips for a religious zealot.* Susan had told me that those kind of shoes were called fuck-me shoes. "On the assumption that you didn't want to order them in quite that way to a saleslady at Filene's," I had said, "what else

57

would you call them?" Susan had said that she'd simply have to find some and point. She'd never heard them called anything else. Probably called hold-my-hand shoes here.

The receptionist returned and smiled and said Mr. Owens would see me. I followed her down the hall and she ushered me into one of the cubicles. There was a gray metal desk and two gray metal chairs and a file cabinet and a picture of a man, probably Bullard Winston, on the wall. Owens stood and put out his hand.

"Bob Owens," he said.

Owens was tall and trim with sandy hair and some freckles. His hands had large knuckles and they cracked slightly when we shook hands. He had on a seersucker suit and a white shirt and a light yellow tie.

I sat in one of the metal chairs and said, "I am looking for a young woman named Sherry Spellman." I took my license out and handed it across to him. He looked at it, smiled, handed it back.

"Not a flattering likeness," he said.

"It didn't have much of a start," I said.

He nodded. "Sherry is with us," he said.

"Here?" I said.

Owens smiled. "She is with us," he said.

"I'd like to speak with her if I may."

"I'm sorry, sir, that isn't possible," Owens said.

"Why not?"

"She has sought refuge with us. We cannot very well violate her refuge at the first request."

"She's here voluntarily?"

Owens put his head back and smiled and rolled his eyes at the ceiling. "My God, yes. How else would she be here? This is a Christian church."

"Her friend says she was taken forcibly. That's why he hired me."

Owens didn't smile. "That is absurd," he said. "Who is this friend?"

I shook my head. "No need for you to know," I said.

"The charge may well be actionable," Owens said. His face was severe, and with his freckles he looked like an angry child.

"Simple charge to disprove," I said. "Let me talk with her."

"No. I cannot. She has a right to sanctuary. She has a right to come here and be undisturbed."

"I appreciate that. On the other hand, you can probably appreciate why I can't just take your word for it."

"I'm afraid you'll have to."

"There are several ways to do this. But the

easiest would be to talk with your boss. May I see him?"

"Mr. Spenser," Owens said. "This is harassment, and it is intolerable. Sherry Spellman is here of her own volition, she is well and happy and does not wish to be bothered. That is the end of it. You'll have to leave."

"Another way would be I could call the cops," I said.

Owens pushed a button on his multibutton telephone and in ten seconds the frizzy-haired receptionist stuck her head in the door.

"Ask Corey to send a couple of men down here, please, Miss Chase."

"Yes, sir," Miss Chase said, and pulled her head out and closed the door.

"Or I could get up and go out and begin to look through the buildings," I said. "See if she is here."

"I have requested two church deacons to come by and escort you from church property, Mr. Spenser. I'm sorry to be so brusque, but we do not turn the other cheek here. And we do not accept intimidation. And we believe in direct, immediate, and vigorous action when necessary."

There was a knock and Owens nodded and two large young men came in wearing white short-sleeve shirts and chino pants. They were both obvious body builders. One had a crew cut, the other was balding, though he was still in his twenties, and combed the sparse brown hair over the bald parts. Vanity even here.

I said to Owens, "I will need to see Sherry Spellman and talk with her. And I will. But busting up your deacons this morning doesn't seem like the way to go about it." I stood up. "I'll be in touch," I said. No one spoke. I walked past the deacons and out of the church. They followed and stood on the church steps and watched me as I drove away.

CHAPTER 10

I drove back down Route 114 to Middleton Square and had a cup of coffee in the Blue Bell Restaurant. It was 10:45. Across the continent Susan would be putting on her makeup now, and spraying some perfume on herself and making sure her hair was perfect. I looked at my reflection in the window. My hair wasn't perfect. Neither was I.

I had more coffee and a piece of cherry pie. I didn't much care for getting pushed around by a couple of overbuilt Jesus freaks. No point in starting a fight. Except to relieve some of the aimless hostility that simmered almost at the border of repression. But that was personal, and it wouldn't do anything for Sherry

Spellman. I wasn't sure it would do anything for me. It wasn't a good time for me to be hostile. I felt not so much weak as slow. And getting beaten to the punch by some guy who combed hair over his bald spot would not make me feel better.

The woman behind the counter said, "Want another piece of pie?"

"Sure." Maybe if I ate enough my energy level would rise. Maybe I was suffering from low blood sugar. It was pretty good cherry pie.

I tried to concentrate on Sherry Spellman and the Bullies. My concentration wasn't what it used to be either. I could try to go over Owens's head. I could talk with Bullard Winston. If you're going over a head, you may as well go all the way over. If that didn't work, I could always go back to basics. When in doubt, sit and watch.

There was a pay phone outside the Blue Bell and a phone book that hadn't been ripped loose. I looked up the Bullies and called the main number.

"Bullard Winston, please."

"Who's calling, please?" It was a pleasant female voice with overtones.

"My name is Spenser," I said.

"May I ask the reason for your call, sir?"

"I'd like an appointment to speak with Mr. Winston."

"Reverend Winston does not normally make appointments."

"I'm looking for a missing girl," I said. "I have been told that your organization is holding her captive."

"Thank you for calling the Reorganized Church, sir," she said, and hung up. Another triumph for smooth talk. I got in my car and drove back up toward the Bullie compound. I parked across from the entrance and sat. Other than Sherry Spellman, I didn't know what I was looking for. I just watched. Some cars came and went. People went in and out of the church. People went in and out of the bungalows. A group of people came out of the church together as if there had been a service, or a class. Various dogs nosed around the shrubbery or slept in the sun, sprawling on the warm gravel of the drive. At noon a large number of people went into one of the bungalows, and being an experienced investigator I surmised it was the dining hall and they were having lunch. I saw no sign of duress. No plaintive screams for help, no leg irons, no automatic weapons. Not even a beret or a fatigue jacket. The place looked like a pleasant religious community. *Clever disguise.*

Periodically one of the three identical blue

Ford Escort station wagons that were parked beside the church would crank into life and drive out of the compound and up or down Route 114. Sometimes there was only a driver. Sometimes the car would have passengers. They were always driven by a deacon in what I realized was the deacon's costume. White short-sleeve shirt, chino pants. At three in the afternoon the whole community turned out on the green and did an hour of calisthenics led by the kid with the crew cut who had watched me off the property that morning. I didn't see any sign of Sherry Spellman, but I was too far away to be sure, especially since I was working from a photo of her, face only. On the other hand, if she were locked away in a dungeon, it wouldn't much matter what photo I had.

I sat until it got dark and didn't see much else. At five everyone went to the dining hall. At seven everyone went to the church. At eight everyone went into their bungalows. I went home.

I had some Irish whiskey for supper and watched the ballgame and when I felt sleepy and dull enough I went to bed and slept badly.

CHAPTER 11

The sky gets light around 4:30 in July in Boston and by 5:15 or so the sun is up. I lasted in bed until six and got up feeling cumbersome and slow, like a stone. Paul was on the couch, so I was quiet making coffee. The air-conditioner in the living room made enough noise to muffle my sounds and I turned on the early morning news while I sipped orange juice and waited for the coffee.

At seven I was lumbering along the Charles, and at 8:15 I was heading north over the bridge to look at the Bullies some more. When I left, Paul was still sleeping.

The commuter traffic was all in the other direction and I was parked by the church

compound before nine. So far in two days effort the only thing I'd got out of this was two
pieces of decent cherry pie. I had some coffee
in a paper cup and I sipped it and watched the
life of the Bullies unfold placidly before me.
Everything was as before. The small station
wagons came and went. The gardens were
weeded, people went in and out of the
church. A little before noon a smoky-rose-
colored Lincoln sedan pulled into the drive
and stopped in front of the church. There
were two buggy whip antennas on the rear
bumpers and a small one on the top of the
trunk. I'd been thinking of getting some.
Made your car look so official. People came
out of the church and from the bungalows.
They stood in a silent circle around the car. A
tall guy in a dark suit and a white shirt got out
of the front and opened the rear door. Stewart Granger got out. *King Solomon's Mines*,
setting out on safari. He had on a crisp khaki
safari shirt and matching slacks, and he carried a thick blackthorn walking stick. He
moved slowly along the circle of Bullies,
speaking to people, touching them on the
shoulder. They dipped their heads as he
talked to them, not a bow, but a kind of rever-
ential nod. When he had worked the circle,
Stewart went up the church steps and into the
church. The people stood outside and

67

watched the door he'd entered and appeared to say nothing. Probably wasn't really Stewart Granger. Probably Bullard Winston. He looked like the picture on Owens's wall.

At noon he went to the dining hall. At 1:10 he came out and got into his car and drove back down Route 114. I copied down his license plate number. Maybe it would be a clue. A little after two o'clock one of the little station wagons pulled out and I followed it. I wasn't learning much sitting. Motion at least gives you the illusion that you're going somewhere.

We went down Route 114 to Route 62 and east to Route 1, and headed north on 1. Twenty miles north of Boston, in the upper reaches of Megalopolis, milk cows grazed in hilly pastures. Northern Essex County looked much as it must have in the eighteenth century. At least long stretches of it still did as the two-lane road meandered north among loose stone walls and white barns and wide tidal marshes with the marsh hay harvested in neat round beehive stacks.

I followed the Ford Escort wagon through Newburyport and over the Merrimack River and into Salisbury. North of Salisbury Center the Escort pulled into the dirt driveway of a frame farmhouse that had been shingled in beige asbestos with a fake wood pattern. The house was surrounded by vegetable garden for maybe 100 yards on each side. Stretching to a roadhouse on the left that advertised "All Country/All Day" and an auto salvage yard on the right, behind the house, were the tidal marshes. Close to the road a small shack with a sign that said FRESH EGGS, FRESH VEGETABLES, ORGANICALLY GROWN. There was a young woman in jeans and a print blouse tending the inventory. It was too early in the year for much except eggs. Hens were not seasonal. They could probably ovulate at will.

One of the khaki deacons got out of the Escort, carrying what looked like a small mail sack. He went into the house, came out in maybe three minutes still carrying the sack, got back into the Escort, and we headed back to the founding church in Middleton.

The courier was easy to tail. He didn't expect to be followed. I was driving a nondescript-looking Subaru hatchback with a four-wheel-drive option for winter crime-stopping, and it looked like most of the cars on the road. I drifted along two or three cars back. Normally tailing was very automatic and gave me time to think. Today I didn't think. I hadn't been able to think much since Susan left; instead, I realized I had been concentrating on balancing the dull ache. If I was careful, I could keep the ache from turning into

69

despair. Across the road on my left a Weima-
raner hunted the marsh flat, coursing back
and forth, its nose to the ground, its short tail
quivering with excitement. Beyond the dog,
in the distance, was the rim of shoreline and
the quality of open emptiness beyond. I'd
never figured that out. It wasn't that you
could see the ocean exactly, but you knew it
was there. The Escort was getting a little far
ahead and I passed a Chevy wagon with kids
in the back making a V sign at me. It had no
meaning anymore and the kids probably
didn't know why they made it. But two fingers were better than one.

We passed Governor Dummer Prep School
on the right. White buildings, a soccer field. I
had noticed in the last few weeks that there
was a kind of rhythm that, if one were careful,
could be controlled. It was easy to lose the
rhythm, but if one concentrated, one could
stay in it and avoid sharp suffering. Keeping
the rhythm also provided you with something
to do. Gave you a kind of purpose in life, getting by without spilling over. A man needs a
goal.

CHAPTER 12

I followed the courier car for the rest of the
week. It seemed as good a way as any to get
some sense of location and activity among the
Bullies. I located a substation in Wilmington,
another one in Lakeville, and one in West
Boylston. The driving was a useful way to pass
time, it required little concentration but of-
fered some distraction. If things didn't work
out between me and Susan, maybe I could
catch on someplace as a chauffeur.

Saturday morning I was back out in front of
the main church.

*I'll give it today, finish out the week, and
tomorrow I'll start nosing around the substa-
tions.*

Good idea.

At about 9:15 one of the small station wagons came down the drive. There were two deacons in it today. They pulled out onto the highway and stopped right in front of me. And got out.

Oh-ho.

It was the same pair of body builders who had ejected me the first visit I made. The one with the thin hair combed over his bald spot was wearing horn-rimmed sunglasses. The one with the crew cut said, "Get out of the car, please. We'd like to speak with you."

I got out and leaned against the car with my arms folded on my chest.

Crew Cut said, "You've been hanging around here for several days."

It didn't seem to be a question so I didn't answer.

"You've been asked," Crew Cut said, "not to interfere in our religious practices."

Still no question.

The bald one said, "So this time you're being told, not asked."

I could feel the quick hot spurt of anger. The exterior and objective part of me was surprised. *Well, well, there is anger in there.*

I said, "Is that actually your own hair you've got pasted down over your scalp or does somebody paint it on for you each morning?"

72

He flushed. Sensitive. His buddy said, "You are very close to getting yourself in some real hot water, pal."

The anger had enlarged and was working its way up from the pit of my stomach, spreading along my back and shoulders and down my arms. I could feel my face getting hot. I was careful with my voice, easing it out so it was steady.

"This is different business," I said, "from pumping iron. It's a business I'm almost sure to be better at than you are. Don't make a mistake." The muscles in my neck and shoulders were starting to bunch on their own. My whole upper body was tense.

The crew-cut deacon said, "You are going to have to be taught a lesson."

He put his left hand out toward me and I hit him with the back of my right hand as I unfolded my arms. I hit Baldy with the front of the same hand. His sunglasses flew off and the genie was out of the bottle. The energy release was immediate and large. It fed itself and intensified as it enlarged so there was only the welter of fists and elbows and knees and feet and forearms. Only butting heads, only gouging and biting, only force expanding in a kind of ecstasy, a frenzy released.

It was over too soon. A shame in a way to waste the energy. The deacons weren't that

73

good. I stood with my chest heaving and the sweat soaking my shirt, staring at them sprawled on the roadway. I had broken at least one arm, and shattered at least one knee-cap. When they woke up they'd be in pain.

"My fuse is awful short these days," I said. "Not your fault."

I got into the car and drove up the gravel drive and stopped in front of the church. Bob Owens was standing in the doorway.

"Your deacons will need medical attention," I said. My breath was still coming in short rasps. "And maybe if I don't find Sherry Spellman pretty soon, you will too." I let the clutch pedal out and the car continued around the circular drive and back out onto Route 114. In the rearview mirror I saw people hurrying toward the road.

The Incredible Hulk doesn't have a girlfriend either.

CHAPTER 13

The deacons had landed a few punches. When I woke up in the morning I had some bruises and my left eye was half shut. My hands were sore. I stumbled out into the kitchen and put ice cubes in a bowl and ran some water and put my hands in to soak. Paul wasn't home. He was in Connecticut with his girlfriend for the weekend. I took my hands out of the ice long enough to start the coffee and squeeze some orange juice and drink it. Then I soaked them some more and held some ice against my eye. I got dressed and poured some coffee and thought about breakfast. That seemed too complicated for me. So I had a corn muffin and drank a lot of coffee and read the *Globe* and the *Times* and half watched *Sunday Morning* on CBS. By 11:30 I was through both papers and felt over-coffeed and there was a Mass being broadcast on TV. It was too early to start drinking. I could go and look over one of the branch churches in Salisbury or West Boylston or Lakeville. Nice choice of locations. No trouble parking at any of them. I thought about that for a while and found it more complicated than what to have for breakfast. I decided to wait until Monday. I looked at the clock, it was 11:33. There was a ball game on television at two and when that was over it would be late enough to start drinking, and then it would be time for bed. The immediate problem was getting through the next two and a half hours. I went into the living room and looked out the window. That wasn't as much fun as I'd hoped it might be.

The phone rang. It was Hawk.

"How are you," he said.

"I'm all right," I said.

"You feel like a date?"

"With you?" I said. "For crissake, you're colored."

"Always figured that bothered you," Hawk said. "So I got a girl in mind for you, she just split with her old man."

"She go for middle-aged thugs," I said.

"She go for me," Hawk said.

76

"Okay, I'll give it a go."

"She'll meet us tonight, six thirty at the Bay Tower Room. I'll bring Laura."

"The Harvard professor."

"Yeah. Your date's a friend of hers. She say something hard, I explain it to you."

We hung up. *A date. Whoopee. Hope my acne doesn't flare up.* I put on my gun and went downstairs. Bullard Winston's registration number had gotten me his address and it seemed a good way to spend a few pre-date hours on a Sunday afternoon. I walked up Arlington to Commonwealth and then west on Commonwealth toward Kenmore Square. Winston's home was in the block between Fairfield and Hereford, a block and a half this side of Mass Ave. It was a graystone town house and it was elegant. The stairs leading up to the front door were broad marble slabs. There were columns rising three stories to the roof on either side of the entry and the big windows above the entry on floors two and three were as tall as a man and paned with violet glass. The front door was black with a very large brass knocker. The glass panels on either side of the door were also violet. I knocked with the knocker. In maybe thirty seconds the door opened and there was Stewart Granger. He wore dark gray slacks and a white broadcloth shirt with the cuffs rolled up and the collar open. White hair showed at the open collar of his shirt and a small crucifix on a gold chain was around his neck. His thick silver hair was brushed back and his face had a healthy outdoor color. He smelled of bay rum, and his smile was open and honest and full of magnetism. Through the open doorway the air was cool. Central air-conditioning.

I said, "My name is Spenser, Mr. Winston, and I've been assaulted by a couple of your church deacons."

He raised his eyebrows. "Reverend," he said.

"Excuse me. Reverend Winston. I've been assaulted by some of your deacons. The press is after me for details. The police are after me to press charges, my lawyer wants me to sue. But I'd rather talk with you and see if we can't avoid trouble."

"That seems sensible, Mr. . . ."

"Spenser," I said again. "With an *S*, like Edmund Spenser."

"The poet," he said.

"Yes," I said.

"Well, come in," Winston said. "Perhaps we can have a cool drink and a chat and work out whatever seems to be the matter."

"Thank you," I said, and he ushered me in.

It was a long high hallway paneled in walnut. We turned right and went into a cool greenish room full of plants. One wall was glass that extended the length of the room and arched up to form a curved glass roof eight feet or so out beyond the room. The floor was polished flagstone and the furniture mostly wicker. There was a small fountain in the glass extension and several of the plants were so tall that they shaded us. The glass was tinted green so the sun didn't penetrate and the air-conditioning could do its work.

"Sit down, Mr. Spenser. A glass of white wine perhaps, or a glass of ale?"

"Ale is fine," I said. I sat in a green-cushioned wicker chair. Winston sat on a wicker sofa, green-cushioned as well, and crossed his legs and touched a button on the end table near his right hand. He was wearing soft burgundy-colored Gucci loafers and no socks. His ankles were tan. A maid appeared in one of those maid outfits that you see in the movies.

"Two glasses of ale, please, Peggy," Winston said. The maid departed. Winston took a long-stemmed briar pipe from a rack on the end table and began to fill it from a leather-covered humidor on the coffee table. The house was very quiet. When Winston got the thing packed to his satisfaction he fired it with one of those little jet flare lighters that pipe smokers use and he was getting a good draw going when the maid came back with two open bottles of Old India Pale Ale on a tray, and two tall glasses. She set the tray down on the coffee table between us and poured some ale into each glass, getting a good head on it, then she left. Winston exhaled some smoke, took his pipe from his mouth, picked up a glass of ale, and gestured at me. I picked up my glass. We both drank. Winston put his pipe back into his mouth, made sure it was going good, and said, "Now, what is this business about assault."

"Well, sir," I said, "I was just sitting in my car outside your founding church grounds up in Middleton and these two deacons came out and attacked me."

"And you had to protect yourself," Winston said.

I nodded.

"You did so successfully," Winston said. "Both men are hospitalized."

I made a sympathetic cluck.

"You had been parked outside there for several days. You had followed our courier vehicles when they went out. Previous to that you were making inquiries about a member of the church community from Mr. Owens."

"That's true," I said. I sipped a little more ale. Bitter. Good title for my memoirs—*Bitter Ale.*

"Mr. Owens informed you that the young

woman was quite well and had sought sanctu
ary with us. You were unsatisfied, and you
were asked to leave."

Winston's voice was rich and pleasant. The
smell of his pipe tobacco was rich and pleasant. The house was rich and pleasant. So was
Winston.

"Also true," I said.

"So the deacons were asked to make you
stop what was viewed as harassment. Strategi-
cally that was sound. Tactically it was an er-
ror. You were more vigorous in your own defense than we had counted on."

"For my age," I said.

Winston smiled. "And now you are here,"
he said. "Persistence."

"Better than skill sometimes," I said.

"I believe that's so," Winston said. "But I
am afraid that I must support Mr. Owens. The
concept of sanctuary is a very old one, and no
church can treat it lightly. I believe that your
concern is Miss Spellman's well-being. And I
realize that a man like you trusts visible evidence and little else. Would my personal assurance of her happiness and safety suffice?"

"No."

Winston took his pipe from his mouth and
held it in his right hand and rubbed his chin
with his thumb, the pipe stem pointing

obliquely away from him. His ale grew headless on the coffee table.

"What would satisfy you?"

"See her, talk with her, alone."

"And perhaps to take her by force and, as the phrase has it so elegantly, de-program her?"

"No," I said. "If she's where she wants to be, she can stay."

"Then I'm to trust you?"

"We'll trust each other. We'll work out a set-up where I see her alone, but in view. If she wants to leave, I walk out with her and you can see that it's voluntary. If she wants to stay, you bring her back and I can see that it's voluntary."

Winston puffed on his pipe. He did it expertly and the smoke floated gently away on the cool silent air. He nodded his head and smiled gently.

"It has a nice symmetry," he said. "But why should I agree to it? It is not our normal stance to compromise."

"Because I'll drive you whacko if you don't. I will find her. If she wants out, I will take her out. I'm sort of at loose ends these days, I got nothing else to do, and I am in a state of advanced ill humor. You'll be my hobby, take my mind off my troubles. In short, I will be a dreadful pain in the ass, Reverend, until I have this straightened out."

Winston smoked his pipe some more.

"Do you have a business card, Mr. Spenser?" He seemed able to keep the terror out of his voice. I didn't seem to scare people as much as I used to.

I gave my card to Winston.

"I'll call you tomorrow," he said. "And discuss what we've decided." He stood up. Dismissed.

We walked to the door. He told me he was glad I'd stopped by. Then he opened the door and closed it behind me. On Commonwealth Avenue I looked back at the house. The porch and the marble steps and the three-story façade with its violet windowpanes were rich and pleasant too. I wasn't.

CHAPTER 14

The Bay Tower Room is not in a high crime neighborhood. It is thirty floors above the city and looks out through floor-to-ceiling glass past the Custom House Tower at Boston Harbor. There is a lot of polished brass and gleaming oak, and an orchestra with a swing era sound. Hawk and Laura were there already. My date was not. Probably still home primping, maybe getting advice from her mom on how far to go on the first date.

Hawk wore a white linen summer suit and a blue and white striped shirt and a white silk tie. A blue show handkerchief poked out of his breast pocket. Laura had creamy skin and red hair. She wore a green summer dress with small white figures in it.

Laura said, "Hello, Edmund." She always called me Edmund, just as she always called Hawk Othello. She probably had cats she called Damon and Pythias.

Hawk nodded at me. I sat down.

Laura said, "Katie will be a little late."

I looked around at the room. "Elegant," I said. "Last blind date I had we took a six-pack to the drive-in."

"How are you feeling," Laura said.

"Fine," I said.

Laura put a hand on my arm. "Come on. It will not be good if you keep it all in."

Hawk grinned. "Laura been reading Dr. Brothers again," he said.

Laura ignored him. "How are you really, Edmund?"

I felt a little spurt of anger. "Suspended," I said. "As in suspended animation."

"I think you should talk about it. It will help you."

The waitress came and we ordered.

"I do talk about it," I said. "But not with everyone."

She looked a little startled.

"I talk with him about it." I gestured with my chin toward Hawk. Laura looked more startled. "And with a friend of mine named

85

Paul Giacomin. What I could actually use is practice not talking about it."

"Othello talks?" she said.

"Hard to believe, isn't it?" I said.

"Oh," Laura said. "Here's Katie."

Hawk stood. So did I. Katie had skin the color of a gingersnap and black hair worn long and a big charming smile. She was wearing a rose-colored jumpsuit tight at the ankles. Laura introduced us.

Katie said she'd heard a lot about me. I said I hoped she didn't believe most of it. We ordered a round of drinks. Katie asked me what my sign was. Hawk made a funny noise, and put his hands over his mouth and coughed.

"Down the wrong tube," he said when he stopped coughing. His eyes were very bright.

"I don't really know my sign," I said.

"I'm a Virgo," she said.

I nodded.

The captain came and took our food orders. The band played "Moon River." Katie was a reporter for a UHF station in town. The food came. One of Spenser's laws of dining is that in high restaurants the food never lives up to the view. I tried my dinner. Right again.

"Have any of you been able to get a real handle on the punk rock phenomenon?" Katie said.

Hawk's face was as amiably expressionless

as it always was. But his eyes seemed to gleam brighter and brighter. He had a bite of lamb. "Can't say's I have," he said.

Laura said, "Well, clearly it is a creature of the tension it creates between itself and the orthodox world."

I nodded.

The band played "Blue Velvet."

We all danced.

"You are a big one, aren't you," Katie said.

"Yes."

We had dessert.

Laura said that she would love to interview Hawk and me together sometime. She had a theory about poetry and violence that she wanted to try out on us.

We had some brandy.

Hawk looked at his watch. "Time to go," he said. "I gotta bookie I gotta threaten early tomorrow."

We all smiled. And got up. And went.

87

CHAPTER 15

I met Sherry Spellman at the International
Food Fair at the Liberty Tree Shopper's Mall
in Danvers. Owens brought her and four deacons came with him. I didn't recognize any of
the deacons. Fresh troops. The food fair was a
semi-circle of fast-food shops around a seating
area full of tables. Owens and the deacons sat
at a table near the Philly Mignon shop and
Sherry joined me near Paco's Tacos.

She was pale blond and somewhat sun-
burned. Her hair was short and she wore no
makeup. She sat down opposite me, folded
her hands quietly on the table before her, and
waited.

I said, "Would you care for coffee, or something to eat?"

She shook her head. Her glance drifted over to her churchmates, and then back to me.

I said, "You know who I am?"

She nodded.

I said, "How are you?"

"Fine."

She had a small voice.

"Are you happy?"

"I'm at peace," she said. Again her glance drifted to the deacons and back.

I said, "Look at me. See how big I am?" I opened my coat. "See the gun?" I took my license out and showed it to her. "See, I am a licensed private cop." She looked at me and nodded. "Now, if you want to leave with me, you can. Owens and the deacons can't stop us. And if you leave with me, I'll protect you as long as you need it."

She nodded.

I said, "Would you like to leave with me?"

She shook her head.

"Tommy Banks says you were kidnapped," I said.

"No," she said. It was the firmest sound she'd made. "No, I wasn't."

"No one tied you up and took you away?"

"No."

89

"You joined the church on your own?"

"Yes."

"Why?"

"Too much hassle," she said. "I had to get away."

"Who was hassling you?"

She shrugged and shook her head. "Everyone."

"Tommy?"

She nodded.

"Who else?"

She shrugged. "Dancing was too hard."

"What was the hardest part?" I said.

"Tommy."

"A slave driver?"

"He . . . it was just that he wanted me to care about it more than I did. Him too."

"What did you want?"

"To be by myself. To see what I am."

"You need the church for that?"

"Yes."

I leaned back a little in my chair. She glanced over at Owens and the deacons. Good name for a country rock group. *Now with their number one single it's Owens and the Deacons. Yeah!*

I shook my head slightly. Concentration wasn't what it should be. Sherry certainly didn't seem frightened. She didn't seem happy either, but her glances at the deacons were more the way a child looks to a parent than anything else.

"Tommy wants you back," I said.

"No." Very firm. Almost animated. "No."

"What's the best part of being where you are?" I said.

"I don't have to worry."

"About what?"

"About anything. Everything is simple and . . . and I don't have to think about things all the time."

"Do you love Tommy?"

"I guess so, I'm not sure. But I can't be with him."

"Too much pressure?"

"Yes."

"Pressure to dance?"

"Pressure about everything."

"Maybe you should move to San Francisco," I said.

"Huh?"

"Private humor," I said. "You don't seem happy."

She shrugged.

"On the other hand, I wasn't hired to make you happy. I was hired to find you and rescue you. But you don't seem to need to be rescued."

She shifted in her chair. She looked at

Owens and the deacons. Her hands still rested, folded, on the table before her.

"Where are you living?"

"Will you tell Tommy?"

"No."

"Salisbury."

"In the branch church on Route One?"

She nodded.

"Between the roadhouse and the salvage yard?"

She nodded again.

Owens and the deacons sat silently watching us across the room. All five men had their arms folded. Uniformity.

"I might come visit you now and then, Sherry. Not to hassle you. Just to visit. See if you need anything."

She nodded.

"You won't mind?" I said.

"No."

"Okay. You may as well rejoin your party."

We stood. Sherry walked quickly back to Owens and the deacons. I went too.

"She says she wants to stay," I said to Owens. "I believe her."

"I should hope so," Owens said. The deacons all sat poised, like I might kick one of them at any moment.

"I told her I'd come visit occasionally. She said that was all right."

Owens didn't say anything.

"If I come to visit and don't find her, I'll start looking again. And I'll be really mad."

I couldn't watch all four deacons at the same time. The one I was watching didn't blanch.

Owens said, "Let's go," and they got up and left. Owens and the Deacons. Actually Sherry and the Deacons sounded even better than Owens and the Deacons. I went out to the parking lot to find my car.

Sherry and the Deacons. Do-wop!

CHAPTER 16

I sat with Tommy Banks on the only two chairs in his studio, in a corner, near a window that looked out onto Huntington Avenue, in case anyone wanted to. We sipped coffee from paper cups. On the other side of the studio the dance company took a break. I had already begun to realize that dancers almost always moved and made little step motions even as they rested. It was as if they were always hearing music, always carving shapes in space.

"She says she wants to stay where she is, Tommy," I said.

"Of course she does, they've brainwashed her."

94

"No. I don't think so. She says she wasn't kidnapped, and that she's free to leave."

Banks's hands were clasped in front of him, forearms on the knees. His knuckles were white.

"They've made her say that. They took her and brainwashed her. I was there, they came and took her and tied and gagged her and dragged her away in the trunk of their car."

Across the room a complex short rattle sounded as someone did a tap step, someone laughed. I kept watching Banks.

"Do you know where she is?" he said.

"Yes."

"We've got to get her out of there. I'll go with you, we'll rescue her."

"Tommy, I don't think she's a prisoner. She has a right to stay there if she wants to be there."

"She doesn't have the right to kill me," he said. His voice was tight and squeezed. "She can't kill me. I can't make it without her. I can't . . ." He shook his head. I knew he couldn't talk. There were tears in his eyes.

"I can't . . ." He tried again. "I . . ." And then he sat with his hands clenched together, and his body hunched forward. I felt like sitting that way too. I straightened up a bit to make sure I wasn't.

"They've taken her away from me," he said. "You can't let them."

He didn't look up. I didn't say anything. Across the room the dancers moved less, and their talk died down. Banks's shoulders shook.

I said, "I'll talk with her again, Tommy."

He nodded. The room was dead silent now. I stood up and walked away. No one said anything. Paul's face was serious as he looked at me across the room. I looked back at him and we both understood something at the same time. There was nothing to say about it, so we didn't speak.

I went on out and down the stairs to the street. It was a clean summer day, even on Huntington Avenue. I walked downtown, past Symphony Hall, toward Copley Square. At the Christian Science complex a few kids were trying to wade in the reflecting pool and an official was chasing them out. In Copley Square the unfriendly high rise of the Copley Place development loomed up over Dartmouth Street, the heavy equipment cluttered the area and had Huntington narrowed to one lane around the construction site. A lot of trouble. Well worth it though, it would eventually rival the Renaissance Center in Detroit for its sense of open ease and hospitality.

It was a market day in Copley Square and

truck farmers were selling produce in front of Trinity Church. People sat on the low wall along Boylston Street and listened to Walkmans or drank beer or ate their lunch or looked at girls or smoked grass or did all at the same time. I moved on down toward the Common. I was trying to think. Never easy.

I didn't think Sherry had been kidnapped. I wasn't sure whether Tommy really thought she had been or not. What he couldn't do was accept that she'd left him voluntarily. I had seen the clenched refusal to let go in him and I had seen Sherry talk about the pressure he'd put her under and I could guess that she had not so much sought the church as fled Tommy. Escaped maybe was a better word.

My heart was with Banks. I knew how he felt. But the kidnapping was fantasy. Even on three hours sleep I was pretty sure of that. Still, Sherry didn't seem to be having a swell time in the church and the church seemed a little hierarchical to me. I had told Owens I'd check on Sherry periodically and I was going to do that anyway. No real harm in looking into it a little more. Maybe there was a better option for Sherry than the Reorganized Church of the Redemption. Maybe there was an option that would ease some of Tommy's pain, or help him through it. Maybe not. Maybe there was no way to ease pain. No harm to trying. It was something to do. Irish whiskey can only take you so far.

CHAPTER 17

I drove up to Salisbury to see Sherry. There were purple field flowers in bright density all over the meadows along Route 1. I'd looked at them nearly all my life but I didn't know what they were called. That was nothing. I'd been with me all my life and had just started to wonder about that.

Sherry was feeding chickens when I got there. She was spreading something that looked like dry dog food pellets around on the ground and a bunch of white hens flurried about her, pecking at the food. I realized I didn't know anything about chickens either.

She looked up at me and didn't speak.

I said, "Hello, Sherry."

"Hello."

"How are you," I said. She kept distributing the pellets. The chickens kept scuttling around after them.

"I'm fine. I told you that last time I saw you."

"I know. I just like to check. You don't seem especially happy."

"The point of this world is not happiness," she said. "It is salvation."

I nodded. "Tommy is in pretty bad pain," I said.

She stopped scattering the pellets for a moment. "I'm sure he is," she said. "But that is Tommy's pain. I won't take ownership of his pain."

"I don't argue the point," I said. "But it sounds like a recited answer. Tommy loves you."

"Tommy needs me," she said. "That's not the same thing."

"Tell me about life here," I said.

"We have a regular life. Exercise in the early morning, study and instruction in the afternoon."

"What do you do for money?"

"We need very little, the mission is largely self-supporting." She gestured at the poultry. "And we grow vegetables and preserve them. Each of us receives a small stipend."

"From the church?"

"Yes."

"Is there anything you want?" I said.

"No. I'm doing what I want to do. I am comfortable. There is structure without pressure. I have friends."

"Do you contribute money to the church in some way?"

"No. My work and my prayers are what I give the church."

"Where do they get the money?" I said.

Sherry looked at me as if I'd spoken in tongues. She shook her head without speaking. I took a card from my pocket and gave it to her.

"Here's my name and address and phone number. If you need me for anything, call me. Or come see me. I'll stop by again. Do you mind seeing me?"

"No," Sherry said. "I kind of like you."

"Thank you," I said. "I kind of like you too."

Walking back to my car, I was startled to find that I kind of did like her and that I was pleased that she kind of liked me. How unprofessional.

Back in my office I called Father Keneally.

"Where does the money come from in the Reorganized Church of the Redemption?"

"Bullard Winston."

"Where's he get it?"

Father Keneally paused. "Actually, you know, I don't know. I don't know if he's privately wealthy or if he has backers. My professional interest is more directly with the doctrinal aspects of religious organizations."

"He doesn't collect from the members," I said. "He pays them."

"Quite unusual," Keneally said.

"Does he do fund-raisers?"

"I don't know," Keneally said. You could tell it was not something he was used to saying. You could also tell that he didn't like getting used to it either.

After I was through talking to Keneally I walked over to the library and looked up Bullard Winston in *Who's Who.* It didn't tell me anything about his financial stability. His town house was certainly costly, and maintaining a string of church missions and paying stipends to all the church members was bound to be costly. And I didn't believe that stuff about the lilies of the field.

I wandered down to the Kirstein Business Library off School Street behind the old city hall and browsed among the exotica of corporate finance and municipal bond issues for most of the rest of the day. I didn't find out where the Reorganized Church of the Redemption got its money, but I did discover in a copy of *Bankers and Tradesmen* that the

102

Bullies were financing the construction of an office park in Woburn. The church held a 500,000-dollar mortgage. The developer was listed as Paultz Construction Company, Inc. Curiouser and curiouser.

I walked up School Street to the Parker House and had a couple of beers in the downstairs bar and thought about how Bullard Winston and his church could loan 500,000 dollars to a construction company. Maybe just the new kids got a stipend and after a while they had to start paying dues or making tithes or whatever you did when you belonged to the church militant. There were 10,000 Bullies altogether, Keneally had said. Fifty bucks a head would cover the mortgage loan, but then there would have to be money to cover expenses. Not impossible. If you got 100 bucks a year from 10,000 people, you had a million. And since it was charity, you didn't have a tax problem. Still, Sherry said they didn't pay dues, they received a stipend. She said it as if all of them received one.

I looked at my watch, almost six. I thought of seeing Susan and then caught myself and felt that spasm inside that I always felt when it happened. I took in as much air as I could and let it out and stood up and went home to make supper for Paul.

CHAPTER 18

The next morning I was at the Kirstein Library when it opened and I went through several years worth of *Bankers and Tradesmen.* By noon I knew that the Reorganized Church of the Redemption had made construction loans to Paultz Construction Company for about three and a half million dollars. Christian charity. I left the magazines on the table and went out.

I walked up over Beacon Hill on Beacon Street with the Common on my left and the elegant eighteenth-century brick-front buildings on my right. I turned up to Commonwealth on Arlington at the bottom of the Public Garden and in fifteen minutes I was at

Bullard Winston's door again. A man in the deacon outfit I was getting to know so well told me that Reverend Winston was not at home and wasn't expected soon. I said thank you and went back down the steps and crossed the street and leaned against a tree and waited.

I experimented with keeping my mind blank. It wasn't as hard for me as it might be for others, but it wasn't easy. If you weren't careful, you'd start thinking of things. And if you thought of things, then your stomach would hurt again. Maybe I could take up meditation, get into self-hypnosis. I shifted my other shoulder against the tree and refolded my arms across my chest and thought of blankness. Like carrying a very full glass of water up the stairs, Hawk had said. He knew things you wouldn't think he'd know. He seemed immune to pain, yet he knew about trying to balance it. He seemed immune to affection, too, except with Susan . . . I tightened my arms across my chest and got my mind back into its blank balance.

It was nearly quarter to five when the same chauffeur-driven rose-colored Lincoln I'd seen before pulled up in front of Winston's house and the good reverend got out. I walked across the street.

"Evening, Reverend," I said.

Winston frowned at me for a moment and then said, "Oh, Mr. Spenser. Did your chat with the young woman proceed satisfactorily?"

"Yes, sir, it did. But now I wonder if you could spare me maybe five minutes more of your time."

"Regarding?"

"Regarding the three and a half million in mortgage notes you hold on property developed by Paultz Construction."

"I hold no mortgages," Winston said.

"The church does."

Winston looked at me for a good silent period. That was okay, I had my mind so blank I could have taken a nap while he stared. "Spenser, you are becoming a pest."

"Yes, I am," I said. "Thank you for noticing."

"I went out of my way to satisfy your curiosity about this young woman. Your curiosity is, I believe, satisfied?"

"Yes, sir."

"Then why do you concern yourself with the financial affairs of a Christian church?"

"Theological speculation, Reverend. I was wondering about whether it really was easier for a camel to pass through the eye of a needle than for a rich man to enter the kingdom of heaven."

Winston turned without a word and walked up his front steps.

"I take it that's your final answer, Reverend?"

The front door opened, Winston went in. The front door closed. Spenser, master of the probing interview. I walked back down Commonwealth, with the sun behind me. The matter of finance did not seem to be something Winston liked to discuss. Why not? If it was all on the up-and-up, why wouldn't he want to rap about it with a pleasant guy like me? The question contained its own answer. Where did the church get three and a half million to loan to a construction company? And why to only one, and why that one?

I wonder if Susan is dating.

CHAPTER 19

I always enjoyed a reason to go to the State House. The great gold dome gleamed in the summer sun and from the top of the steps you could look down across the Common and feel the density of the old city thickening behind you in time's corridor. I went in and found the Secretary of State's office and got sent to the Charitable Trust Division and without having to kick back to anyone got a copy of the year-end financial statement for the Reorganized Church of the Redemption.

I took the computer printout with me and walked from the State House, across the street past the Robert Gould Shaw monument at the top of Beacon Hill, and down the steps into the Common. There was a lot of skateboarding and roller-skating and Frisbee, and wino. Some Hare Krishna shucked and shuffled down near the Park Street subway kiosk. I found an empty bench and sat down and took off my sunglasses. I put my sunglasses into my breast pocket and looked around me. No one was watching. I put my hand unobtrusively into my inside jacket pocket and came out with a pair of half glasses and put them on. I looked around again. No one seemed to have noticed. I looked down at the printout. *Ah-ha. There it is. I wear these only to see.*

The physical assets of the Bullies were worth less than 300,000 dollars. Their income, from interest on mortgage loans, was 315,000 dollars. If they had three and a half million out, that meant it was loaned at less than ten percent. That was five or six points below market. Of course maybe it wasn't when the loan was made. I got out my small yellow notebook. Time was I could remember everything. Now I had half glasses and a notebook. Next thing I'd have a midlife crisis. A pigeon landed on the ground near my feet and waddled around looking for a kernel of peanut among the littered shells in front of the bench. *Why this is midlife crisis nor am I out of it.* I looked at my notes. The loans were recent. Mortgage rates had not been under ten percent when the loans were made. The pigeon gave up on the peanut shells and flew away on undulating wing. I watched him go. What the printout didn't tell me, and what the notebook didn't tell me, and what Reverend Winston wouldn't tell me was where the Reorganized Church got three and a half million bucks to lend out in the first place.

I took off my half glasses and put them back into hiding. Maybe I should have my sunglasses made prescription and I could wear them all the time and people would never know. They'd think I was cool.

I stood and put on my nonprescription sunglasses and walked back toward my office. In the Public Garden I stopped on the little bridge and leaned on the railing and watched the swan boats move about on the pond and the ducks in solicitous formation cruising after the boats, waiting for peanuts. They could not be fooled by shells. I wondered how ducks knew so quickly the kernel from the husk. One of nature's miracles.

When I got to my office there were two thugs waiting in the corridor. I've spent half my life with thugs. I know them when I see them. They were leaning against the wall in the corridor on the second floor near the elevator just down past my office door. I unlocked the office door and went in. I left the door open. The thugs came in behind me. I walked over and opened the window and turned around and looked at them. One of them had closed the door.

The head thug was bald with squinty eyes and a longish fringe of hair in the back that lapped over the collar of his flowered shirt. There was a scar at the corner of his mouth as if someone had slashed it during a fight and the repair job had not been done by Michael DeBakey. The assistant thug was taller and in better shape. He had black hair in a crew cut and deepset eyes and long wiry forearms with blue dancing girls and twined snakes and daggers tattooed on them. There were four upper teeth missing in the front of his mouth and someone had somewhere in his life obviously deviated his septum.

We looked at each other.

"You guys in the Mormon ministry?" I said.

"You Spenser?" the bald one said.

"Mmm," I said.

We looked at each other some more. A small objective part of me noticed, from the far upper right corner of my consciousness, that I felt almost nothing. A faint lassitude, maybe. No more. Blankness is all.

"Look, you guys, I'm trying to get clammy with fear, and I can't. I know that disappoints

111

you, and I'm sorry. I'm trying, but nothing seems to happen."

The bald one said, "You got nothing to be afraid of if you do like we tell you."

"Or if I don't," I said.

"You do any more messing around with the Reorganized Church then you gonna end up bad dead," Bald said.

I felt something. What I felt was *I don't care*. Just a little flash of *I don't care,* then it was gone and blackness came back.

"You two going to do it?" I said.

"You don't do what you're told, we'll do it."

"You might want to take a number," I said. "There's a waiting list."

"You think we're fucking around, asshole?"

"It's the best you can do," I said.

Bald looked at his partner. "Maybe he needs a sample of what we can do," he said. The partner nodded and looked mean. Bald looked back at me and found that I was pointing my gun at the little indentation in his upper lip, right below his nose. He stared at it.

"Ordinary caliber thirty-eight slug," I said. "No liquid center, no cross-cut in the nose, no magnum load. Nothing special to worry about for a couple of toughies like you."

Both men stared at me.

"I don't suppose you feel like telling me

who asked you to come over here and frighten me to death."

They didn't say anything.

"No, I figured you wouldn't. It's a corny question anyway."

They didn't move.

"It was good of you to show me what you can do. I don't mean to be ungrateful. But if you come back, I'll kill you."

They kept looking past the gun barrel at me.

"Take a hike," I said, and they both turned, together, and left my office. I went and closed the door behind them and then with my gun still in my hand, hanging at my side pointing at the floor, I walked over to my window and looked out onto Boylston and Berkeley streets.

In a moment they appeared on the corner and walked to the car that was illegally parked by the subway entrance. It was a white Chevy sedan. Bald got in on the driver's side and his partner got in the other and they drove away. As they did I wrote down their license number. A trained detective.

CHAPTER 20

Bald's white Chevy was registered to Paultz Construction Company. My finely honed investigative instincts began to sniff the aroma of rat. Bald and his partner were hoods. They didn't do construction and they didn't do Bible study. They did kneecaps. I'd seen too many guys like Bald and his partner to be wrong on that. And it meant that Paultz Construction was dirty. And it meant that the connection between Paultz and the Bullies was something that people wanted to keep secret.

"So what?"

Nobody had hired me to investigate anything like that. Tommy Banks had hired me to rescue his girlfriend and she didn't want to be rescued. I was just killing time. Killing time with Paultz Construction could get me killed.

I don't care.

Across the street my art director was back, bending over her board. She looked up as I looked at her and smiled and waved at me across the street. I waved back. She bent back to her work.

I took the phone book off the window ledge where I kept it and looked up the number of the ad agency and dialed it and asked for the art director. I watched across the street as she picked up the phone and tucked it against her face with her left shoulder.

"Linda Thomas." She continued to work on the board as she spoke.

I said, "My name is Spenser, I'm across the street smiling a winning smile out my window."

She looked over.

"My God," she said. "It's like talking to a pen-pal."

"Would you care to have a drink with me after work?" I said.

"That would be lovely," she said. "Where and when?"

"Ritz bar, this evening when you get through."

"Five thirty," she said.

"I'll meet you there," I said.

She waved across the street again and we hung up. It would feel a bit silly to sit there the rest of the day looking across the street. I got up and went out. It was good weather and I had Susan's book. I went to the Public Garden and sat on a bench near the swan boat pond and read.

A man and woman in their forties came and sat down on the grass near the pond under one of the willows. They had lunch in a big paper bag and shared it, leaning against the tree trunk, their shoulders touching. I dog-eared my page and stood up and walked away, across the Public Garden, toward Arlington Street.

Sherry Spellman didn't belong in an outfit that had connections with Bald and his friend. I couldn't spend the rest of my life reading in the park. I couldn't take her away from the church, but maybe I could take the church away from her. I had one end of someone's dirty laundry and I was going to pull it all out, it was a way to kill time. And it was better to kill time than have it kill me.

From my office I called Marty Quirk. Neither he nor Belson had ever heard of the Paultz Construction Company.

"They're dirty," I said. "I know it."

"Lot of people are dirty. Because I'm a cop I'm supposed to know every one of them?"

116

"Another idol crumbles," I said.

"I'll ask around. I hear anything, I'll let you know."

"Thanks."

"You okay?" Quirk said.

"I don't know," I said. "I'm working on it."

"You need something, you call me."

"Yes."

We hung up. I called Vinnie Morris.

"What do you know about Paultz Construction Company?" I said.

"Why ask me?" Vinnie said.

"Because they're crooks and so are you. Figured you might have crossed paths."

"Spenser," Vinnie said. "You got a big pair of balls. Last year Joe Broz and I discussed aceing you. Now you call me up and ask for a favor."

"What are friends for, Vinnie?"

Vinnie laughed a little.

"I don't know a goddamned thing about the Paultz Construction Company."

"Ask around," I said. "You hear anything, let me know."

"Maybe."

Hawk came into my office. I hung up the phone.

I said, "Hawk."

He said, "Want to eat? Or start drinking early?"

"Eat," I said.

Hawk was wearing a pink suit with a pale blue shirt and a pink and blue small-dotted tie. A blue show handkerchief was tucked into his breast pocket and his head gleamed in the sun. As we walked along Berkeley Street no one made any comment on his appearance. No one seemed to think a pink suit was sissy.

We turned up Newbury. "How about Acapulco," I said. "Mexican cuisine."

"Tex-Mex," Hawk said. "I like it."

"It's no Lucy's El Adobe," I said.

"On the other hand," Hawk said, "it's no Guadala Harry's either."

We went up Newbury Street past the galleries and boutiques and stores that sold Danish modern waterbeds.

"You know anything about Paultz Construction Company?" I said.

"Nope."

"Two people driving a Paultz company car came by and told me that if I don't stop looking into the Reorganized Church of the Redemption, they would punch my ticket for me."

Hawk smiled happily. "You faint or anything?"

"Almost, but I managed to get my gun out and point it at them."

"So they decided not to do it right then."

"True," I said.

Acapulco is a small informal restaurant downstairs on Newbury Street that serves decent Mexican food and splendid Carta Blanca beer. We went in. People stared covertly at Hawk.

"The Reorganized Church has loaned the Paultz Construction Company three and a half million in construction mortgages," I said. "What does that sound like to you?"

"That sounds like laundering money," Hawk said.

"Yes."

"I'll see what I can find out about Paultz," Hawk said. "There's people talk with me that don't talk with you."

"There's bad taste everywhere," I said.

"You going to keep doing it."

"Yes. I don't like that kid being involved in something like this."

"Sherry?"

"Yes."

Hawk smiled again. "Thought you wouldn't," he said. "What kind of shape you in?"

I shrugged. Hawk drank some Dos Equis beer.

"People trying to kill you, you got be able to concentrate."

I nodded.

119

"You care if somebody blow you away?"

I watched the bubbles rise in my beer glass. "No," I said.

Hawk nodded. The waitress brought us our food. Hawk ordered another Dos Equis. The waitress looked at me. I shook my head. She went away. The room was half empty and not very noisy. I could feel the weight of Hawk's impassive stare. The waitress brought him his beer. He poured half of it into his glass and watched the head form and then drank a swallow and put the glass down.

Looking at Hawk, I knew why he frightened people. The force in his dark eyes was intensified by the absence of any expression.

"You better move on from there," Hawk said. "See a shrink, read a book, join a church, talk with me. I don't give a fuck how you do it. That your problem. But you don't move on, you gonna get flushed."

I sat motionless and didn't want my food. The beer was going flat in my glass.

"And something I won't do is try to explain to Susan how I let that happen." Hawk said. "Or Paul."

I nodded.

Hawk said, "You want your lunch?"

"No."

"Hand it over here," Hawk said.

I passed him my untouched plate.

"I got a date tonight," I said.

Hawk looked up and smiled a wide smile. "That's a start," he said.

I watched him put away my lunch.

"How come you know this stuff," I said.

"Easy when it not happening to you," he said.

"It is not happening to a lot of people, but they don't know things you know."

"I know what I need to know, babe. Sort of a natural rhythm."

Linda Thomas was five minutes late. Early by the standard Susan had set. She was five foot five and black-haired with eyes that were neither green nor brown but both at different times. She was slim and small-breasted and big eyed with a wide mouth and, especially around the cheekbones, she looked a little like Susan. She was wearing a gray suit with a red print blouse and a kind of full bow at the neck that vaguely suggested a necktie. The print of the blouse was small.

"I'm wearing my power outfit," she said, and smiled and put out her hand. I stood and shook her hand and held her chair and she sat.

"Very professional," I said, "small-print blouse and all."

"Career," she said, "onward, upward. Tell me a little about yourself."

121

I did, and as I talked I discovered that I was telling her more about myself than I had expected to. And more about Susan and our estrangement. By seven o'clock in the still-bright summer evening we were sitting on the grass beside the swan boat pond in the Public Garden leaning our backs against each other as we talked, only very slightly drunk, watching somebody's German short-haired pointer hunt the area, scattering pigeons and treeing squirrels.

"Funny," Linda said, "having a drink with a detective I thought we'd spend the evening talking about crime and instead we spend it talking about love."

"Yes," I said. "I'm a little surprised at that myself."

"That you'd talk so much about love?" Linda said.

"That I'd talk so much about myself."

"You're very open," she said.

"Apparently. But enough about me. Let's talk about you. What do *you* think of me?"

She laughed. "I think that Susan is crazy."

"Or I am. Is there someone in your life?"

Linda said, "I'm separated from my second husband. Almost a year. We see each other and maybe it will work out. But I live alone right now. We've been married seven years."

"How old are you?" I said.

"Thirty-eight."

"Thank God," I said. "You look much younger than that."

"You don't care for youth?"

"From my vantage, babe, thirty-eight is youth. Much younger is childhood."

The feel of her sitting with me, our backs together, in the park, by the water, watching the dog, was righter than I could ever have imagined. I felt odd, as if there were something missing. As if I had set something down.

The pointer barreled past after a squirrel. I said, "Are you hungry? Would you care to eat something?"

"Yes," Linda said. "I have two steaks in my refrigerator. Come to my house and help me cook them."

"It's one of my best things," I said.

Linda lived in a condominium on Lewis Wharf. Which meant she had a good salary or big support payments. We walked to it as the evening settled. Crossing Tremont Street I took her hand, and when we got to the other side I kept it. She rested her head briefly against my shoulder. We stopped along the way and bought a bottle of Beaujolais. Linda's apartment was blond wood and exposed brick, and an all-electric kitchen with a built-in microwave oven. It was modern and bright and clean and surprisingly unhomey. Her stove was a Jenn-Air with a built-in grill that exhausted the smoke and Linda took two steaks out and put them on the grill.

"Can you make a salad?" she said.

"Wonderfully," I said.

Linda pointed to the refrigerator. "Please," she said. "After you fix us a drink."

She took a bottle of Scotch from the cabinet over the stove. It had a long funny Scotch name. "Single malt," she said. "On the rocks for me, with a twist."

I made two drinks and gave her one. The Scotch was remarkable. She took a sip and turned to the steaks. I began the salad. We moved easily about the small kitchen, not getting in each other's way although there was very little room.

The steaks sizzled on the grill. Linda turned from the stove and looked up at me. She was smaller than Susan and had to tilt her head more. She held her drink in her right hand. I looked down into her face, and her eyes were very dark and had a kind of swimming quality.

"This is very strange," she said.

I nodded.

"Aside from looking across the street these years, I don't even know you and yet we somehow fit."

124

I nodded again. She raised her face toward me. I bent forward and kissed her. She opened her mouth and kissed me back, her body arching against me, her left hand pressing me against her while her right held the drink out. The kiss was long and open-mouthed and she moved a little against me as we kissed. When we stopped she stayed against me and leaned her head back to look up at me.

She looked at me silently. "You're intense," she said.

I shrugged. "I'm just at the beginning of trying to figure out what I am."

"You're wonderful," Linda said, and put her face up and kissed me again.

We ate our steak and salad and French bread on a glass-topped table in front of the picture window looking out over Boston Harbor. It was dark now, but one could see ship lights occasionally, and the sense of ocean was inevitable and vast.

"What if Susan has another man?" Linda said.

"Painful," I said.

"Endurable?"

I sipped a little Beaujolais. "We'll see."

She put her hand out toward me. I took it and we held hands silently, squeezing each other, my eyes looking directly into hers.

"I am committed to Susan," I said. My voice sounded rusty. "If I can rejoin her, I will."

"I know," Linda said.

We finished eating our supper. The silence was not awkward. We cleared the dishes and Linda served Sambuca and coffee. We sat on the couch to drink it and Linda turned toward me and stared with her melting gaze at me and then pressed her mouth against mine.

I had never been with anyone like her. In her passion and the wide openness of her abandon, she was breathtaking. Her power suit was in a heap on the floor, tangled with her lavender undergarments and my suit.

We made love on the couch, and on the floor, at one point rolling against the coffee table and slopping our coffee and Sambuca onto the marble surface. Later we were beneath the glass-topped dinner table. Sometime later we went to bed.

Linda lay on her side, propped on an elbow, looking down at me as I lay on my back beside her.

"It would be absolutely idiotic," she said, "to be in love with you having just met this evening."

"I know," I said.

She said something that sounded like "ohhhh" and pressed her mouth against me again and we made love again. She cried out

and dug her nails into my back. Sometimes
we were crossways on the bed, and once we
fell off and didn't pay any attention. Back in
bed, long into the dwindling night, we fell
asleep with our arms around each other. And
I did something I had not done since Susan
left. I slept.

CHAPTER 21

I walked back from Linda's apartment in the hot morning feeling somehow encapsulated, as if a fine high keening surrounded me, and the pavement were undulant and somewhat insubstantial. The space in which I moved seemed crystalline and empty. What I felt was shock. To feel for someone other than Susan what I had felt for Linda was so startling that the world seemed unlike the one I'd walked in yesterday morning. The Quincy Market area was nearly empty at that time of day. Newly scrubbed and shining, its shops and restaurants freshly open, full of promise. Hopeful.

In front of my apartment on Marlborough

Street, Vinnie Morris was parked on a hydrant, the motor idling, the windows of his TransAm rolled up. He lowered one of them.

"Get in," he said, "we'll have breakfast."

I got in the passenger side. Vinnie raised the window and the air-conditioning took care of what little warm air I had brought in with me.

"You look like you been out all night," Vinnie said. He was a medium-size man, very compact, very neat. He had a thick black mustache and he smelled of musk oil, though modestly.

"Yes," I said.

We drove around the Public Garden and down Charles Street. Vinnie jammed the TransAm up onto the sidewalk on the corner of Charles and Mt. Vernon streets and we went into the Paramount Restaurant. I ordered whole wheat toast, Vinnie ordered steak and eggs.

"Breakfast is important," Vinnie said.

I nodded. "Got to keep that cholesterol level up."

Vinnie said, "Aw, bullshit."

We brought our food to a table, and sat.

I drank some coffee. The world still echoed strangely around me, and the intrusion of Vinnie, the intrusion of the world in which I worked and lived, was jarring. Vinnie with a

129

gun, Vinnie who spoke for Joe Broz, or killed for Joe Broz, was for me the ordinary, the workaday. I felt as if my footing were unsure, as if the earth were slippery.

"You were asking about Mickey Paultz," Vinnie said. He drank some coffee and put the cup down. His movements were careful and economical and precise. His nails were manicured.

"Yes."

"Tell me a little about why you want to know."

"I'm looking into a religious group called the Reorganized Church of the Redemption. I notice it has made a number of large low-interest loans to the Paultz Construction Company."

Vinnie was watching me carefully. He nodded.

"After I had asked the head of this religious group about the loans, about where they got money for the loans, a couple of meanies came around and told me to butt out, or else."

"Scared you right off, didn't they," Vinnie said.

"They drove off in a car registered to Paultz Construction."

"Don't mean Paultz is dirty," Vinnie said. "Maybe these guys were just a couple of shovel operators on a slow day. Maybe Paultz is buddies with the church guy."

"These were hoods, Vinnie. And the thing is, the church shows no visible source of income. Where they get the money to lend Paultz?"

Vinnie cut into his steak. "The faithful?"

I shook my head. "No. They receive money from the church, not the other way around."

"Church pays them to be members?"

"A stipend, for work," I said. "So where's the money come from?"

Vinnie smiled his careful smile and chewed his steak. He ate in small bites, chewing thoroughly. He swallowed. "You have a theory," he said.

"I say Paultz is dirty, he's making dirty money, and he's laundering it through the church."

Vinnie nodded. "Makes sense. He makes money under the table, donates it anonymously to this church, they lend it back to him at a low rate. He invests it at a higher one, or uses it to build property and sells it at a profit, and the money he gets is shiny clean. Maybe Joe will found a church."

Vinnie ate some more. I drank my coffee and ate half a piece of toast.

"Heroin," Vinnie said.

I was quiet.

131

"Mickey Paultz processes most of the skag that gets sold in New England," Vinnie said.

"How nice for him," I said. "Where does he do the processing?"

"Warehouse on the construction lot."

"You folks do business with Mickey?"

"You want to do dope business, you do it with Mickey. We do, Tony Marcus does, Worcester, Providence."

"Would it break your heart if someone put Mickey away and left the business up for grabs?"

Vinnie smiled. "Nature hates a vacuum, buddy boy."

"And so does Joe Broz."

Vinnie patted his mouth with a napkin.

"Joe says you need some help on this, we'll help, up to a point."

"Why don't you just waste Paultz," I said. "And move in, sort of like a proxy fight?"

Vinnie shrugged. "Mickey's connections are good," he said. "Joe don't want to do it that way."

"So he wants me to do it," I said.

"He wants it done. You called us, you know. We didn't call you."

"If I do this right, maybe I can get my own territory," I said. "Couple of junior high schools . . . 'hi, kids, I'm the candy man.'"

"I don't like it too much either, tell you the

132

truth," Vinnie said, "but Joe don't always check with me on these things. Joe likes dope. And you and me both know if Mickey Paultz don't do it, and Joe don't do it, then somebody else will do it."

"So I take Paultz out, Joe moves in, and I look the other way."

Vinnie smiled and jabbed his right index finger at me. "Most definitely," he said. "We get what we want, you get what you want, and all the junkies get what they want. What could be better?"

I shook my head. "Hard to imagine," I said.

CHAPTER 22

Wearing a pair of chino pants and a short-sleeve white shirt I went to call on Mickey Paultz. I had bought the pants a couple of years ago in case someone gave me a pair of Top-Siders and invited me to Dover. The shirt I'd had to buy for this occasion, but it was a business expense—disguise. I was undercover as a deacon. Since deacons didn't go armed that I could see, and since I didn't go unarmed, I'd strapped on a .25 automatic in an ankle holster. A quick draw is not easy with an ankle holster, but it was better than nothing.

Paultz Construction Company was on the southern artery in Quincy, a big sprawling ugly lot full of heavy equipment surrounded by chain link fencing with barbed wire on top, with an office trailer near the front gate. Back in the lot was a big prefab corrugated steel warehouse. I pulled the Ford Escort wagon that I had rented into the lot outside the gate and went through the gate and into the office. If the two sluggers who called on me were there, I'd simply turn around and leave. But I figured they wouldn't be. They didn't belong out front where the customers would see them. I was right. There was a fat woman in black stretch pants and pink blouse manning the typewriter and answering a phone.

When she got through on the phone she looked at me and said, "What do you need?"

"Mr. Paultz," I said.

A long unfiltered cigarette was burning in an ashtray.

"He's busy," she said.

The phone rang, she answered, talked, hung up.

"I'm from Mr. Winston," I said. "I have to see Mr. Paultz."

She took a drag on her cigarette, put it down. "I don't know any Winston," she said.

"Ask Mr. Paultz," I said. "He'll want to know."

She shrugged and got up and went in through a door into the back half of the

135

trailer. In a moment she came back and said, "Okay, go on in," then she sat down and picked up her cigarette. I went through the open door and closed it behind me.

Mickey Paultz sat in an overstuffed chair with a piece of paisley cloth thrown over it. He looked at me and said, "What's up?"

He was thin with short gray hair and rim-less glasses. A kitchen table was next to the chair and on it were two phones and several manila folders.

"Mr. Winston has to see you," I said. "He can't call. He thinks the phones are tapped. There's real trouble he says and wants to meet you in City Hall Plaza near the subway as soon as you can make it."

Paultz's expression didn't change. "Okay," he said.

I waited a minute.

Paultz said, "You want something else?"

A man of few words, I said, "No," and turned and went out.

I drove straight to Boston and parked in front of the precinct station on Sudbury Street by a sign that said POLICE VEHICLES ONLY, grabbed a camera, and hotfooted it across the street to the Kennedy Building. Hawk was there near the funny-looking metal sculpture.

"Winston go for it?" I said.

"Unh-huh." Hawk pointed with his chin across the vast brick plaza in front of City Hall. By the subway kiosk on the corner, Bullard Winston stood glancing at his watch and shifting his weight lightly from one foot to the other as he waited. He was wearing a seersucker suit. I sighted my camera at him and focused through the telephoto lens.

"Paultz coming?" Hawk said.

"I'm not sure," I said. "I told him my story and he said okay and sent me away."

"If he don't come, we gotta think of something else," Hawk said. "Can't pull this gig twice."

"I know." Behind the funny-looking sculpture I kept the camera steady on Winston.

"That him?" Hawk said.

Paultz got out of a white Chevy sedan that double-parked on Cambridge Street with the motor running.

"Yes," I said. As Paultz came into my viewfinder I snapped pictures of him and Winston talking. They talked for maybe fifteen seconds before Paultz turned and glanced around the plaza. We stepped out from behind the funny-looking sculpture. I kept snapping pictures, Hawk put two fingers in his mouth and whistled. Both Winston and Paultz turned and stared. Hawk waved. I had cranked out maybe twenty pictures. I stopped and rewound the film. I took out the roll and slipped it into my pocket. I let the camera hang by its strap from my right hand and Hawk and I began to walk across the plaza toward Paultz and Winston.

Paultz turned and spoke to someone in the Chevy. The doors opened and the two sluggers got out. Hawk was wearing an unconstructed silk tweed summer jacket and he unbuttoned it as we walked across the plaza.

"Oh, to be torn 'tween love and duty," I said, " 'sposin' I lose my fair-haired beauty."

"Those the two that threatened to do you in?" Hawk said.

"Yep."

"Fearful," Hawk said.

We stopped in front of the four men. Winston looked uncertainly at Hawk. His face was narrow with fear. Paultz looked the same as he had in his office. Except taller. Standing he was maybe six four.

"How's the weather up there," I said.

Hawk chuckled softly. Paultz said, "I want the film."

"I don't care what you want, Mickey," I said. "I got pictures of you and Winston together. I know you are washing money through his church, I know you process and distribute heroin out of your warehouse. And I want you to deal with me."

Without a word Winston turned and began to walk rapidly away toward Tremont Street. Hawk looked at me. I shook my head. Winston kept going.

"You give me the film or we take it," Paultz said.

"In City Hall Plaza? A block from Station One?"

Hawk said, "Couldn't take it anyway. Even if we in Siberia."

"Do we talk?" I said.

Paultz looked at me and at Hawk blankly. Then he said, "No," and turned and walked to the white Chevy. The sluggers went too. They got into the car and drove away.

"I think Mickey just told us to stick it," I said.

"I think Mickey know there's more than one way to skin a cat," Hawk said.

"I think he knows that too," I said.

"And you the cat," Hawk said.

CHAPTER 23

I had contacts made of my pictures at a fast service place in Harvard Square. I chose the best pictures and had half a dozen 81/2 by 11 glossies made up. I put four of them in a safe-deposit box, kept one of them for Mickey Paultz, and took the other one with me when I went to call on the Reverend Winston.

When he let me in he looked sick. And sleepless. Much of his calm elegance had gone.

"What are you going to do?" he said when I came in.

I handed him the photograph. "I'm going to negotiate with you," I said.

Winston stared at the picture.

"No matter how long you look at it," I said, "it is still going to be a picture of you and Mickey Paultz."

"It doesn't prove anything," Winston said.

I slammed my palm down on the tabletop. Winston jumped. I said, "Come on, Bullard. You are through and you know it. I know what's been going on. I can tie you to Paultz and it's only a matter of time before the cops or I can prove it in court." It was a trick I learned on the cops. Call them by their first name, makes them feel less important. Bullard didn't seem to feel at all important. He pressed his clenched hands against his mouth and stared down at the picture.

I lied to him. I said, "I'm not after you, Bullard. I'm after Paultz."

He raised his eyes toward me. Salvation.

"You lay it out for me, all of it, how it worked. How much money, where it came from, how much you got off the top for the laundry job, all the things you know."

"If I do?" he said.

"Like I say, I'm not after you."

If he'd been smarter, he'd have known I was lying. My ploy to get them pictured together was warning enough for Paultz to eliminate anything incriminating on his lot or in his business. I didn't care. Whether Paultz ran the heroin store, or Joe Broz, or Harry the

141

horse, made very little difference to me or to the junkies whose lives would be forfeit to it. What I really cared about was Sherry Spellman.

"I'll tell you all I know," he said. And he did.

I took notes and when he was through I let him reread my notes and had him sign each page. He did without protest, although I could tell that seeing it written out on paper made him nervous. It was about as I had it figured, although the numbers were higher than I'd guessed. One thing I noticed was that as far as I could tell there was only Winston's word on the Paultz connection, which meant if Winston were dead, there'd be no real way to tie Paultz to any of this. If I knew it, Paultz knew it. I went to Winston's desk and used his phone. I left word with Henry Cimoli for Hawk to call me, gave him Winston's number, and hung up.

"I'm going to wait here for a call," I said. "Did anyone else in your organization deal with Paultz?"

"No."

"You're the only one that knows where the money comes from?"

"Yes."

"How'd it start?"

Winston stared out through the glass at Commonwealth Avenue. "The first donations

142

were anonymous," he said in a flat soft voice. "Big donations when we were struggling to get a foothold. Life-saving donations."

"Seed money," I said. "It's the same way they develop a junkie."

"Then one day Mickey Paultz came and called on me. He introduced himself, explained that he'd been the anonymous contributor, and made another donation. In cash, always cash. No strings. That continued for a while and then he came again and asked for a loan. I was sorry, embarrassed even, but I explained to him that I'd spent all of his donation money on church business. He said that was understandable, that he'd give me a very large donation and ask me to lend that to him. I was puzzled. Naive, I suppose, but I couldn't see why he'd want to do that. He insisted, and I said that I had never seen anything done like that, and that I felt I should consult an attorney before I did it."

Winston paused and hunched his shoulders a little.

"Then Paultz explained it to me. He told me where the money came from and why he had given it to me and said that I'd be through if people knew it was dirty money."

"And?" I said.

"And there'd be no more donations if I didn't go along."

143

I nodded. "Hard to give up," I said. "The church, the power, the home, the car, the deacons, the whole thing."

"I couldn't," Winston said. "I couldn't give it up. I'd created it, built it, made it work, made it flourish. I couldn't."

We were both quiet until the phone rang.

I answered. It was Hawk.

I said, "I need a body guarded. Can you take the first shift while I work up some more troops?"

"Winston?"

"Yes."

"Paultz?"

"Unh-huh."

"Wondered when you'd think of that," Hawk said. "I be along."

When I hung up, Winston looked at me and licked his lips.

"What is this about a bodyguard?"

"You're the only one who can tie Paultz to this," I said. "He'd sleep better if you were dead."

Winston said, "Oh, my dear God."

"It's all right," I said. "Hawk will keep you safe for now, and I'll arrange with a man I know to give you round-the-clock protection."

"Is Hawk the Negro who told me Paultz had to see me?"

144

"You."

"The one who was with you when you took the pictures?"

"Yes."

"He'll guard me alone?"

"He could guard Yugoslavia alone," I said.

"I could have some deacons come."

I shook my head. "If there's trouble, they'll just get hurt," I said.

Winston nodded. There was no resolve left in him. He was scared and it made him weak.

In ten minutes Hawk showed up at the front door carrying a leather gun case and a Nike gym bag. He nodded at Winston, took a box of 12-gauge shotgun shells from the gym bag and set them on the table, put a box of .357 shells beside them, unzipped the gun case, took out an Ithaca shotgun, loaded it, and leaned it against the table. Then he looked around the room.

"Good place to get shot from the street," he said.

I nodded. Winston seemed to sink back deeper into his chair. He looked smaller than he had when I'd first met him.

"Let's find an inside room," Hawk said. He put his ammunition back into the gym bag. Picked up the shotgun.

I said, "I'm going out and work on things. I'll be back to give you a break."

Hawk nodded. Winston looked at me as if I were his father leaving him at a strange nursery school. "Do what Hawk says," I told him. "You'll be fine."

He nodded. I left him with Hawk and let myself out the front door.

I went to my office and called Vinnie Morris. He wasn't there. I asked for Joe Broz. There was no one by that name there. Which was a crock, but Joe had always been shy. I left word for Vinnie to call me and hung up and sat.

Across the street there was something hanging in Linda's office window. I looked harder. It was a big red heart. I smiled. The phone rang. It was Vinnie.

"For crissake, don't you know better than to ask for Joe," he said.

"Self-amusement," I said. "You still want to help me on the Paultz thing?"

"Depends."

"I need some people to keep Bullard Winston alive."

"The minister or whatever the fuck he is?"

"Yes. He's all we've got on Mickey."

"You with him now?"

"No. Hawk's got him."

"He's safe enough for now," Vinnie said, " 'less he annoys Hawk."

146

"How about you pick it up at eight o'clock, give you time to organize it."

"Sure. Where is he?"

I told him. "I'll be there at eight to meet you. Come yourself so I'll know they're your people."

"No sweat, just make sure you don't jerk us off on this one, buddy boy. We do this and you don't dump Paultz and Joe is going to say it ain't cost-effective. You understand?"

"Would I mislead you, Vinnie?"

"Yes," Vinnie said. "But only once."

I said, "See you at eight," and hung up.

Before I left the office I drew a large smile face on a piece of typewriter paper and taped it into my window facing Linda's heart.

CHAPTER 24

I made some Xerox copies of my notes of Winston's spilled beans. I put a copy in the safe-deposit box, took out one of the photos, and went back to my office. I got out two manila envelopes. In each I put a copy of the notes and a picture of Paultz and Winston. Then I went to see Sherry Spellman.

She was wearing jeans and a sweat shirt that said DO YOU KNOW JESUS across the back, and was hoeing beans in a garden in back of the Salisbury branch of the church. She stopped when she saw me and looked a little less serious. Life would never be bubbly for Sherry.

We sat in the front seat of my car and I showed her the picture first.

"Reverend Winston, you recognize. The other man is Mickey Paultz, whose primary source of income is the processing and sale of heroin."

Sherry looked at me and widened her eyes. I gave her the notes. "Notice," I said as she began to read, "that each page is signed by Reverend Winston."

She read on and then stopped and looked at me and read some more. When she got through she shook her head.

"No," she said.

I nodded.

"No. He wouldn't have done this. I don't know what you're doing but it's not true."

I waited. There was the hum of locust in the air, and the sound occasionally of a dog, and now and then the rush of a car past us on Route 1.

"Why does he say these things?" I said.

"He didn't. You made them up and forged his signature." She looked at me. I waited.

She shook her head again. Her eyes were wet.

"No," she said. "You wouldn't do that."

She began to read the notes again. Halfway through she put her head down in her hands and began to cry. I patted her shoulder softly.

149

Finally she stopped crying. "It's true," she said. Her voice was clogged.

"Yes," I said. My throat felt a little achy.

Sherry hunched very tightly, her shoulders pressing in toward her small breast. "Isn't there anyplace for me?" she said.

"You like this church?" I said.

She nodded. "I know you think it's junk," she said. "But it is home for me. It is peace. We're not crazy cults or anything. We love God and trust Him and try to live like Jesus. And now it's gone." She was crying again. "And now I have no place."

I held her against me. My breath was heavy balanced against her sobs.

"It's not gone," I said. "I'll fix it for you."

A crowd of chickens came around the side of the building clucking and pecking at the ground and began to mill around the yard near the front door. Feeding time. Sherry's body shook as I held her.

"I'll fix it," I said. "You don't need Winston. You are the church, not him."

She tried to speak, but she cried too hard. It wasn't intelligible.

"You can run it," I said. "I'll get you financing. I'll get you help."

A young woman in a plaid shirt and a wraparound denim skirt and cowboy boots came out of the front of the church building and began scattering feed to the chickens. They made a lot of noise about it. As she scattered the feed she looked uneasily at me and Sherry in my car.

Sherry stopped crying. She sat up and wiped her nose with the sleeve of her sweat shirt. "How?" she said.

"You'll see," I said.

"Do you really know how?" she said.

"Yes, but it's better if I not tell you."

"You really know?"

"I have a plan," I said.

CHAPTER 25

I left Sherry with the confession and picture, back in the envelope. I took the other envelope and drove down to Quincy to visit Mickey. This time when I went in the two sluggers were there along with Paultz.

I tossed the manila envelope on the desk. The squinty-eyed one was chewing a toothpick. Nobody spoke. Paultz picked up the envelope and looked at the contents. He read my notes of Winston's spilled beans. Then he put the picture and the notes back into the envelope and put the envelope on the table next to a dirty white coffee mug that said Canobie Lake Park on it in red letters.

"This is going to get you killed, pal," Paultz said to me.

"Yeah, but only once," I said.

"You got copies of this shit," Paultz said.

I didn't comment.

"But that's all you got," he said. "And when Winston's dead you'll have even less."

I waited.

Paultz sucked a little on his lower lip. "And when you're dead you'll have nothing at all."

"Be restful though," I said.

"You're going after a very big fish with a very goddamned small piece of bait. It doesn't make sense."

Paultz took his rimless glasses off, and plucked a Kleenex from a blue flowered box on the table and polished the glasses and put them back on.

"I'm missing something," he said. "What do you want?"

"I want a trust fund," I said. "One million dollars."

"Too bad," Paultz said. "I heard you were different. That you weren't a chiseler." He shrugged.

"It's for the church."

"Winston's church?"

"Yes."

"There ain't a million in my whole operation."

153

"Then I take you down too," I said.

Paultz smiled faintly. "You think you can do that? You think anyone can find any evidence around here of anything but the construction business?"

"I have Winston's confession."

Paultz nodded at the table where the envelope was.

"That won't stand in court, you know goddamned well it won't. And Winston will be dead, so he can't testify."

"And some of your customers will talk," I said.

"Who?"

"People you wholesale to."

"Name one."

I shook my head.

"And what happens to them when they testify?"

"They get immunity from prosecution," I said, "and you go away and they take over the company."

Paultz looked at the ceiling. He sucked his lower lip again.

"Could be Marcus. The big nigger with you today could be from Marcus."

I didn't say anything.

"And you could be full of shit," he said.

Which was getting rather close to home. I had no idea if Broz would let anyone testify

154

with or without immunity. I had no idea if anyone would give anyone immunity.

"And if I go for the trust?" Paultz said.

"I leave you in place."

"You don't care if I push junk on helpless children," Paultz said.

"Someone will," I said. "You're no worse than the next piece of dog shit that would run your business."

The squinty-eyed slugger said, "Your mouth gonna get you hurt bad pretty soon."

I kept looking at Paultz. "What say, Mickey, want me to get a trust drawn up?"

"Two hundred and fifty," Paultz said.

"Five," I said.

"Three fifty," Paultz said.

"I'll get it drawn up," I said.

Nobody said anything else. I left.

CHAPTER 26

"I have a friend," Susan said on the phone, "a guy friend."

I felt vertigo way inside. I said, "Yes."

"I've known him for a while," Susan said. "Before I left."

"In Washington?" The vertigo spiraled down. Bottomless.

"Yes. He's from here. And he got me this job."

"He must be a fine man," I said, "or you wouldn't be with him."

"I don't live with him," Susan said. Her voice was steady but I could hear strain in it. "And I don't wish to live with him or marry him I have told him that I love you and that I will always love you."

"Is he content with that?"

"No, but he accepts it. He knows that he'll lose me if he presses." The firmness in her voice was chilling.

"Me too," I said.

Silence ran along the 3000 miles of line and microwave relay. Then Susan said, "You have got to get over Los Angeles. That's not a condition, or anything. It is truth. For your own sake. You have to be able to fail, to be wrong. For God's sake, you are human."

"Yes," I said. "I'm trying. I met a woman, and she helps."

"Good," Susan said.

"What's his name?" I said.

"You don't know him, no need to name him. He is not part of you and me."

I said, "That cuts it pretty fine."

Susan was silent.

"You don't mind Linda?" I said.

"No. You have to unlock. You have to open up. You're like a fortress with the drawbridge closed. If Linda helps you, I like it."

"And it makes you feel less guilty," I said.

"Maybe, and maybe if there's someone with you, I worry for you less . . . sometimes I worry about you so that I can barely breathe."

"I care about her," I said. "I guess I sort of love her. But not like I love you. Linda knows that. I have not lied to her about it."

"The only thing that would be awful," Susan said, and I knew from her voice that she was speaking of things she'd thought about often, "would be if you said to me, 'I never want to see you again. I never want to look at your goddamned face again.' When I think of that I get the awful anxious feeling in the pit of my stomach."

"I will never say that," I said.

"Maybe you should use words like *never* and *ever* less often," she said.

"I'll never use them ever again," I said.

"Weak humor," Susan said, "but better than none."

"It hurts only when I laugh," I said.

"Yes. I'm going to hang up now. You be careful of yourself."

"I will."

"I'll call soon."

"Yes."

She hung up and the silence in the room swarmed in on me. I looked at my watch, 10:30. Linda had gone to a meeting of the art directors of Boston. I called her. She was home. I went. It was raining again.

Linda was wearing a pink nightgown when she let me in. I put my arms around her and held her against me soundlessly. After a while she leaned her head back and looked at my face, her body still pressed against me.

"Susan?" she said.

I nodded.

"Come to the bed," she said. I hugged her harder against me.

She said it again, gently. "Come to the bed. We'll lie on the bed together."

I went with her to the bedroom and we lay on the bed. I hadn't even taken off my rain-coat. Linda kissed me for a long time. And she touched my hair and rubbed the back of my neck. And patted my cheek quietly and kissed me again.

I clung to her as if I clung to earth, as if to let go were to disperse into the rainy night.

Linda seemed to know that. She held me as I held her and kissed me and patted me. There was no sexuality to it. There was love and need and solace.

She said, "Do you want to talk?"

I shook my head.

She rubbed my neck some more.

"You talked with Susan," Linda said.

"Yes," I said. "She has a friend."

Linda gently disengaged us and put her hands on each side of my face and looked at me from very close and said softly and slowly

159

with emphasis, "So do you," and kissed me on the mouth, and now it was more than love and need and solace. Now there was sexuality.

Raincoat and all.

CHAPTER 27

Vince Haller drew up a trust agreement for me that was twenty-eight pages long and read like the Rosetta Stone.

"They give courses in gobbledygook at law school?" I said.

"Law school is gobbledygook," Haller said. "No need for a special course."

"If it had been written by a sentient being, what would it say?" I was in Haller's office in the penthouse suite at 5 Staniford, thirty-eighth floor. Genuine antiques, original oils, Oriental rugs, word processors, good-looking secretaries, twelve attorneys. There was gold in gobbledygook.

"It would say that all earning of the capital

161

funding of this trust would be paid to the Reorganized Church of the Redemption, in the person of Sherry Spellman, or her designee, and successors in perpetuity. It would say further that money deposited to this trust was deposited irrevocably."

"Who administers the trust?" I said.

Haller smiled. "Me," he said. "Or my designee and successors."

"Fee?"

"No fee," Haller said. "A tax deductible donation of time at our standard billing rate will be made each month." He was wearing his trademark white suit and a wide maroon knit tie with a gold collar pin.

"So all I have to do is get the thing funded and we're in business."

Haller handed me a deposit slip. "Got the account all ready. Opened it with a one-hundred-dollar tax deductible donation of my own. Checks should be made out to the Reorganized Church of the Redemption Trust."

"I have a feeling that the deposits will be in cash," I said.

Haller shrugged. "Always a negotiable instrument," he said. "You want to come out to the house for dinner Sunday? Mary Margaret has been on my ass to invite you out."

I shook my head. "Thanks, Vince, but I can't make it Sunday."

Haller nodded. "How are you?" he said.

"Still here," I said.

"I got a bottle of Black Bush," he said, "that I brought back from Ireland last time. Want to drink it with me and talk a little?"

"No," I said. "I talk too much as it is."

"How alone are you?" Haller said.

"Paul's with me, and I see Hawk a lot."

Haller shook his head.

"And I've met a very wonderful woman," I said.

"They're all wonderful," Haller said.

"Well, many of them," I said.

"I love them," Haller said. "The way they talk, how they smell, the way they touch their hair, everything."

"I know," I said.

"I never thought one woman was enough," he said.

"I've always thought it was."

"Mary Margaret shares your view," Haller said. He stood and took a bottle of Bushmill Black Label Irish Whiskey from an antique highboy, poured two shots, and came around the desk and handed me one. "They don't export it, you know," he said. "Got to buy it in Ireland."

We drank.

"Mary Margaret's a fine woman," he said. "Good mother, good wife." He grinned. "Du-

163

tiful lover. But I got a girlfriend in Cambridge that the nuns never got to." He drank some more whiskey and shook his head. "Twenty-six years old, knows things that surprise even me, and I've been researching the field for some years."

"You love your wife?" I said.

"Sure." Haller came around the desk and poured more whiskey into my glass. "Best of all, but I love the girlfriend, too, and I know a woman in Washington I love, and I have loved five or six other women in the last five or six years."

I drank some of Haller's whiskey. It made Murphy's taste like Listerine. "Worth the trip to Ireland," I said.

"Yeah, it's wonderful, isn't it. You love this woman you've met?"

"Yes."

"Surprise you?"

"Yes."

"You'll learn," Haller said. "You still love Susan?"

"Yes."

Haller smiled happily. He nodded. "See? See? Already you're learning." He filled his glass and pushed the bottle toward me across the desk. His phone rang. He picked it up and listened and said, "Tell him I'll get back to

164

him, and Alma, hold all my calls, will you, honey?" He hung up.

"Maybe I loved a woman in Los Angeles," I said. "At least a little."

"Sure you did, why not give her a buzz? Never can tell when you'll get to L.A."

"She's dead," I said.

"The broad you were body-guarding?"

"Yes."

"Took the firm six months to get that straightened out with the L.A. prosecutor's office too," Haller said. "I didn't realize she mattered to you that way."

I looked at my whiskey, the light from the window made the amber look golden when I held it up. I drank some.

"I'm not sure I did either," I said.

165

CHAPTER 28

Vinnie Morris had promised two men on Bullard Winston around the clock and whatever else Vinnie was, he was good for what he said.

"Vinnie tell you something you can take it to the morgue," Hawk said. I nodded.

We were driving down the southern artery toward Paultz Construction. I had my short-barreled .38 in a hip holster, Hawk was like an MX dense pack. He had a .44 magnum in a shoulder holster, a .32 automatic in his belt, and a 12-gauge double-barreled shotgun with the barrels sawed off and most of the stock removed. It was lethal at four feet and useless at twenty.

"You got a razor in your shoe?" I said.

"Sho' 'nuff, boss," Hawk said. "Jess wait till yo turns yo haid."

"None of you people do a good black accent," I said. "Didn't you ever listen to *Amos 'n' Andy?*"

"Not unless they yelled in my window," Hawk said. "We didn't have no radios where I grew up."

We pulled up in front of Paultz's yard.

"You think he gonna let you hoist him like this?" Hawk said.

"Yes. He doesn't know what I've got. He doesn't know who's in this with me. Three hundred and fifty thousand is zippidy-do-dah to him. It'll buy him some time to find out how much of a threat I am."

"He gonna kill you, babe. Now or later."

"If he can," I said.

We got out and walked toward the trailer. Hawk carried the shotgun in his right hand, slapping it gently against his leg as we walked. He might have been carrying a salami for all the attempt he made to conceal it.

The fat woman was not in the outer office. Leaning against her desk was a barrel-bodied man with an army .45 stuck in his belt in front. He jerked his head toward the door to the inner office and we went on in. Paultz was there sitting in his armchair, and the two thugs I knew were there, and a white-haired man in an expensive suit was there sitting in the other chair by the kitchen table. He had a briefcase. One of the two thugs, the younger one with the tattoos, was holding an M-2 carbine with a banana clip.

I said, "I'm going to take an envelope out of my inside pocket."

Paultz nodded. I took out a number ten envelope and handed it over to Paultz. "The original," I said, "of Winston's confession."

Paultz took it and handed it to the white-haired man. The white-haired man opened it and read the confession. He had healthy pink skin. When he finished reading he nodded at Paultz.

"How do I know you haven't copied it?" Paultz said.

I shrugged. "You're paying me not to show them around."

"You still got Winston?" Paultz said.

"Of course I do. That's why you're going to give me money. So I won't use him."

"How about he talks on his own?" the white-haired man said.

I looked at Paultz. "What do you think, Mickey?"

Paultz shook his head.

"Correct," I said. "Give me the bread."

The room was quiet. Hawk tapped the shotgun rhythmically against his leg. Since we'd walked in the room he'd looked steadily at the two thugs.

I said, "Don't screw around with this, Mickey. You know you're going to do it, so let's get it done."

Paultz looked at me silently, then he looked at the white-haired man and nodded. The white-haired man handed me the briefcase. I took it and turned and walked out. Hawk came behind me. We got into the car and drove away.

"He's going to kill you," Hawk said.

"Count the money," I said.

"It'll be right," Hawk said. "No point short-changing you now."

"I know, but count it anyway. Don't want to embarrass myself at the bank." Hawk put the shotgun on the floor, took the briefcase, opened it, and started counting.

I drove straight to the branch of the First National Bank near Haller's office. It was in Charles River Park Plaza on Cambridge Street. I parked. Hawk closed up the brief-case.

"Look like three hundred fifty thou to me. In big bills."

We went in and deposited it to the Reorganized Church of the Redemption Trust account. It took a while but bankers will, finally, still accept cash.

Back in the car Hawk said to me, "Now what?"

"Now," I said. "We double-cross Paultz."

CHAPTER 29

The Reverend Bullard Winston and I sat in a conference room in State Police Headquarters at 1010 Commonwealth Avenue and talked about Mickey Paultz. With us was a large mean AFT cop named Riordan, a state cop named Devane from the state organized crime squad, a scruffy narcotics cop from Quincy named McMahon, an assistant prosecutor from the Norfolk County D.A.'s office named Rita Fiori, and Martin Quirk.

Ms. Fiori said, "I'm not clear what interest Boston homicide has in this affair, Lieutenant Quirk."

"Unofficial," Quirk said. He jerked his head

at me. "I know Spenser and he asked me to set up this meeting."

Ms. Fiori crossed her legs. She had elegant legs. "Then I think our first order of business is to establish jurisdiction." Her tailored suit fit well around the hips.

Riordan sighed. McMahon, the Quincy cop said, "Rita went to Harvard."

Rita smiled at him. "And one of the things I learned there, Artie, is that a case needs someone in charge of it . . . and it shouldn't be some asshole narc."

Winston sat in something like a trance as the discussion of who was in charge roiled around us. He was pale, his shoulders slumped, his breathing was shallow. He sat motionless for the full half-hour of discussion that finally resolved in Devane, the statie, being acclaimed case coordinator. When it had been settled Devane looked at me.

"Okay," he said. "Let's hear from you."

Devane had a neat mustache and looked a little like Wayne Newton.

I said, "My associate, Reverend Winston here, will give you a full statement detailing the way Mickey Paultz laundered money through the Reorganized Church of the Redemption."

McMahon murmured, "Saints preserve us."

"And I will produce the names of two wit-

172

nesses who will, if granted immunity, testify under oath that Mickey Paultz sold them heroin in wholesale amounts clearly intended for resale."

Devane said, "Who are the witnesses?"

"First the immunity," I said.

"We can't do that without even knowing who they are," Fiori said.

"That's the deal," I said.

"Where'd you come up with these witnesses?" Devane said.

Beside me Winston remained motionless, looking at the floor. A vein pulsed in his right temple. Otherwise he might have been dead.

I shook my head.

Quirk said, "Off the record."

I looked at Devane. He nodded.

"Joe Broz," I said. "Broz gave them to me."

"Broz?"

"Yes, Vinnie Morris actually, but you know when Vinnie talks, it's Joe's voice."

Devane nodded again.

"Can we trust them?" Fiori said.

"We can trust them to say what Vinnie told me they'd say."

"Are we suborning perjury here?" Fiori said.

"Probably," I said.

Fiori smiled at me. Her teeth were even and white, her hair was reddish-brown and fell thickly to her shoulders. Her eyes were enormous and blue and innocent. "But in a good cause," she said.

"Yes, ma'am."

"What's Broz get out of this?" Devane said. I shook my head.

Quirk said, "He eliminates a competitor."

Devane said, "And maybe replaces him."

Quirk shrugged. "One creep at a time," he said.

They were quiet then, Riordan sprawled in his chair, his frame too big for it, his legs stretched out in front of him, his arms folded over his chest. Rita Fiori bit her lower lip, and looked at Devane. He looked at Riordan, Riordan nodded. Fiori nodded. Devane said, "Okay, immunity."

I took an envelope out of my coat pocket and handed it to Devane.

"Names," I said. "They'll come in with their attorney whenever you want. His name's there too."

Devane opened the envelope, looked at the names. Passed the envelope around. "Anybody know them?" he said.

McMahon said, "I do. Both of them."

Fiori looked at Winston. "Hadn't we ought to get a statement from the Reverend Winston?" she said.

Devane pushed a tape recorder across the

conference table closer to Winston. "We'll tape what you say," he said. "And transcribe it and give you a copy of the typescript. Do you wish an attorney present? You have that right."

Winston looked at me. I shook my head. Winston said, "No." His voice sounded dry and out of use. He cleared his throat.

"You understand," Devane said, "that you are not receiving immunity."

"Yes."

"Although the judge will know of your help here."

I handed Winston a Xerox copy of his earlier statement. Devane pushed the button on the tape recorder. Winston began to talk, referring to the earlier statement, but supplementing and enlarging, his voice growing stronger as he talked, as if the catharsis of confession had begun to quicken his spirit.

CHAPTER 30

It was Saturday afternoon, and an early August monsoon was upon us. A cool hard rain slanted by a strong summer wind was pounding down at an angle and had been since Friday night. Linda and I drove out to Assembly Square to see *Return of the Jedi* at the movie complex there. There were eight theaters in the complex showing the same eight movies that every other theater complex in the Northeast was showing. The supply of product must be down in Los Angeles.

"It's going to be a very cute movie," Linda said. She was wearing high-heeled boots, tight jeans, and a tan raincape with the hood thrown back. The rain was coming straight into my windshield and the wipers were sweeping not drops but sheets of water off the glass. I was wearing a trench coat and my dark brown low-crowned cowboy hat. With the coat collar turned up I felt very much like Dashiell Hammett on the outside. Underneath I had jeans and sneakers and a black T-shirt that said SLC DANCE in purple letters.

"Cute," I said.

"The first two were adorable," Linda said. "I should think a romantic like you would like them."

"No horses," I said. "I don't like a movie without horses."

The parking lot had been temporarily diminished by construction and it was crowded. I found a slot at the far end of the lot.

"Want me to drop you at the door before I park?" I said.

"No, I kind of like the rain," Linda said.

"Me too." Susan would have wanted to be dropped.

Inside, Linda bought some popcorn and we sat and watched the movie. It took about two hours.

In the lobby, as we shuffled out with the crowd, Linda said, "Now, wasn't that cute?"

"How about silly," I said. "That's almost like cute."

"It was pretty silly, I guess."

177

"Horses," I said. "Horses would have saved it."

It was still raining like it used to in Korea when we went out. On a nice day it would still have been light, but here at 5:15 with the overcast and the rain, cars were snapping on their headlights as we pulled out of the lot. Beyond where my car was parked another car had parked, illegally, half out into the street. Inconsiderate bastard. No need to park in the street. Plenty of spaces open around the lot, now that several of the movies had let out.

Linda took my hand and tapped it lightly against her thigh as we walked. "It's a kind of comic book, isn't it?" she said.

"Yeah, or a pulp magazine." Why would somebody park like that next to my car? It was live-parked, the wipers were going. The car on the other side of me had the wipers going too.

"Absolutely fearless heroes," Linda said. "Absolutely hideous villains. Monstrous tortures. But no sex."

Why would a car be live-parked on either side of mine? Why would two cars sit with the motors running in a theater parking lot at a shopping mall on a rainy Saturday.

I stopped.

Linda said, "What is it?"

"Something's wrong," I said.

The two cars sat there, boxing mine. The wipers going. The theater neon splashed brightly on the shiny asphalt. The taillights of cars were bright and their headlights made glistening sweeps as they pulled out and backed up and shifted into first and pulled away. Home for maybe a supper of baked beans and corn bread. Get ready to go out on Saturday night.

I edged Linda sideways between two parked cars. We stood still. Linda had her hood up, but the wisps of hair that stuck out in front were plastered to her forehead. The rain ran in a small drizzle off the brim of my hat when I tipped my head forward. The two cars didn't budge.

Linda hunched her shoulders impatiently and squeezed my hand. "What are we doing?" she said.

"There's a car parked on either side of mine, with the motors running. It's making me nervous."

"Why . . ."

I shook my head. "Come on," I said. We went down the row of parked cars and swung out wide around the perimeter of the parking lot. The exodus from the afternoon show was over, the influx for the early evening show had arrived and parked and gone inside. There was little movement in the lot. We crossed the street and moved behind the cars parked on that side, moving along the near end of the shopping mall, parallel to where my car was parked and bookended. We stopped behind a Dodge van with the spare tire mounted on a swingaway rack, and some racy stripes swooshed along its side.

"You think those men are after us?" Linda was whispering.

"No," I said. "Me. I think that Mickey Paultz is trying to hit me."

"Shouldn't we call the police?"

"Yes."

I stared at the cars beside mine. Looking through the rain-splattered windows of the van.

"But we're not going to," Linda said.

"Not yet," I said.

"What are we going to do?"

"We'll wait awhile," I said. "See what they do."

Linda tugged her cape tighter around her, the hood over her head, and pressed against the van. "I'm scared," she said. "I'm so scared I can barely stand up."

"I'm sorry," I said. "But I want to keep you with me."

"Because why?" she whispered.

I shook my head. I remembered another rainy day. In Los Angeles. When I had blundered through an oil field. Looking for Candy Sloan.

Linda's voice became more insistent, and her whisper was louder. "Because *why?*" she said.

"I'm not going to lose you too," I said.

"My Jesus Christ," Linda whispered. "They don't want me."

I looked at her in the semidark with her cape clutched to her and the hood tightened around her small face. She was shaking.

"Yes," I said. "They're not after you."

The car on the outside of mine was a light blue Buick sedan with four doors. As we watched, it slipped into gear and moved away from my car and down the aisle toward the theater.

"He's impatient," I said. "He's going to look."

The Buick went down the aisle, turned at the end, and moved slowly up the next aisle. The other car stayed where it was beside mine. It had a maroon vinyl roof and looked like a Mercury or a Ford.

"Okay," I said. "In a minute I'm going for the car. As soon as I do, you head for the mall. Get in there and mingle. These guys don't want you and don't even know what you look like. Once you're away from me you'll be safe."

"Will you come back for me?"

"Yes, I'll meet you in the bar in the mall, Dapper Dan's it's called. If I'm not there by closing, call the cops. Boston Homicide, ask for Sergeant Belson or Lieutenant Quirk. Talk to either of them and explain what happened. If neither is there, talk to whoever you get."

She nodded.

"Sergeant Belson, or Lieutenant Quirk, okay?"

She nodded again.

The Buick was at the near end of the next lane. It turned and headed back down the next one. Crouching as low as I could, my gun in my right hand, the car keys in my teeth, I sprinted across the open road toward my car. I yanked the door open and I was in. And the key was in the ignition. I turned the key and tromped on the accelerator. It started. The window of the inside car started down. I fired at it, shattering my own window on the passenger side. I floored the Subaru and screeched, wheels spinning on the wet pavement, out of the slot and toward the street. A bullet punched through the side window and out through the windshield, sending spiderweb cracks out in a flared radius.

I stuck the gun into my pocket and using both hands headed along the edge of the parked cars, staying close to them for cover, and rammed a right turn and floored it for Mystic Avenue. Behind me the Buick and the other car roared after me. It looked like a Ford.

There was a red light at Mystic Avenue and a Chevy wagon stopped at it. I swung inside it and ran the light, turning right onto Mystic Avenue with the rain driving straight at me. The chase cars behind me parted, one went outside, one went inside the Chevy as they, too, ran the light. There were two more red lights at the complicated intersections of Routes 28 and 93 and Mystic Avenue. I ducked past an oncoming Volvo and heard brakes scream behind me as the two chase cars avoided it. It gave me a fifty-foot longer lead. I U-turned under the sign that said not to under Route 93 and headed back in toward Charlestown. At Somerville Lumber I went up the ramp onto 93 with the Subaru going as fast as it would in every gear. Four cylinders were not many. The car fishtailed on the slippery pavement, but I held its nose in and never let up on the gas. I turned my headlights on. There was maybe a mile of straightaway and the two chase cars were closing the gap with their big engines. Not good. I swung off at the Sullivan Square exit and plunged down into Charlestown. The Buick was hard behind me, coming on my right. The ramp was potholed and the Subaru bounced like an eccentric pony as we careened down the ramp by the Hood milk plant. On the straight-away that ran toward Bunker Hill College the Buick was right up on my tail on the inside and the Ford, if it was a Ford, was only a yard or two back on my left. As we came up on the college I veered left and into the tunnel that led toward City Square. The Buick couldn't make it and screeched past on the surface above me. The Ford went into the tunnel with me at about seventy and when we came back up thirty yards farther on, the Buick was running the light on the surface road but far-ther back. Ahead was City Square. Ahead also was a traffic jam that backed up from the Charlestown Bridge and the light at the Bos-ton end. I swung up onto the margin of the road; my speed dropped to fifty. I yanked the four-wheel-drive lever up and the car trem-bled as it went in. To the right was a rotted chain link fence, ahead I knew there was a gate, and a driveway that led into the sand and gravel business located under the ele-vated structure of Route 93. The fields around it were head-high with weeds, and scrap, and abandoned municipal maintenance build-ings. I was gaining on the chase cars. They were skidding and spinning their big wheels in the muddy roadside, lurching half sideways as they came on. I got to the gate. It was open. I wrenched the Subaru into a skidding turn and rammed on into the mud driveway and across it and in among the weeds that were higher than the car. Among the weeds was a pile of steel girders left over from the demolition of the elevated railroad that used to run into City Square. The Subaru hit them with the left headlight and bumper and fender and tore them loose and canted up on one side as the four-wheel drive kept shoving. The car stalled with one wheel two feet off the ground and the whole left front quarter shredded.

I rolled out with my gun in my right hand and headed through the weeds toward the new Charles River Dam.

The two chase cars churned into the drive through the gate and skidded to a halt behind the now lifeless Subaru, their headlights sweeping the tops of the weeds as they stopped.

I lay flat in the weeds, facing back toward the pursuit, soaked from the parking lot and now the drenched weeds and the mud.

Saturday night is the loneliest night of the week.

CHAPTER 31

The headlights went off, except the one re-
maining on my car. It slanted up like a search-
light. I heard car doors open and close. Then
my headlight went out and it was nearly dark.
There was no attempt at stealth. They knew I
knew they were there. How many? Four at
least, two in each car. Maybe more. There
were traffic sounds all around. Behind me to
the right, City Square; about me, Route 93;
behind me and to my left, the Charlestown
Bridge.

I heard the pump slide back on a shotgun as
someone jacked a shell up into the chamber. I
knew what it was. It doesn't sound like anything else. Linda was in the shopping mall by

now, out of the rain, walking among the shoppers, scared but safe. I wouldn't lose her. They wouldn't kill her on me.

The matter at hand was to see if I could keep them from killing me. I was snuggled into the mud among the weed roots, smelling the harsh weedy smell. I was soaked through, trench coat and all. Still lying in the mud, I shrugged out of the trench coat. It was doing me no good and it slowed me down. Light-colored as it was, it also improved my visibility. The cowboy hat had long since gone. I didn't remember it falling off. They didn't make them like they used to. Tom Mix never lost his.

Around among the weeds were a number of piles of steel girders, of the kind that had done in the Subaru. I worked backward on my belly toward the pile nearest me, and edged behind it and rose to a crouch. I could see the pursuit moving the weeds as they came on. Mostly I couldn't see them, just the wave of the high vegetation. They seemed to have fanned out and were coming in four, or whatever, abreast.

Behind me maybe ten yards was a dirt road that looped sloppily around along the water to my left, and led eventually past where the bad guys were moving, to the sand and gravel yard five hundred yards beyond. It was hedged with the weeds and I could see only a brief patch of it. I thumbed back the hammer on my gun. It was short .38, not good for much range. I rested my forearm on the top of the steel pile and aimed at the movement on the farthest right, and watched. With my left hand I had to wipe the rain from my eyes. Without losing sight of my target I was trying to keep a peripheral sense of where the others were. They didn't know where I was, so they moved very slowly. But it would not be pleasant if I was staring at the right side of the pursuit and someone from the left side came up and shot me in the head.

I could hear no conversation among the pursuit. There was enough traffic sound to muffle it, but they didn't need to talk. They knew what they were doing, and how it should be done. We were at the verge of the harbor, where the Charles emptied into the Atlantic through a series of locks built into a just-finished dam across the mouth of the river. The wet air was strong with the smell of the salt sea, and the faint echo-y sense of moving water. The movement through the weeds paused, wavered, began again, and for a moment I saw a man with a beard. I fired, aiming just below the beard, squeezing the shot off carefully so as not to jerk the gun. I was running for the road when I heard a grunt from the direction of the bearded man and some movement in the weeds. The bass thump of the shotgun coincided with the clatter of shot off the steel pile I had just left. I was on the dirt road running, now straight up, hidden by the weeds, sprinting along the curve that would take me in behind the bad guys. Someone honked his horn above me on Route 93. Then a considerable number of horns began honking. A nation of sheep.

A hundred yards down the road I ducked off it back into the weeds, cut across to an abandoned storage building, crouched beside it and waited, breathing with my mouth open as quietly as I could. There were four bullets left in the .38. I didn't have extras. Usually I did, but Saturday afternoon at a PG movie I had figured five rounds were enough. No such thing as too much money or too many bullets. Live and learn. I hope.

The loading door to the warehouse was open, four feet off the ground, sagging badly on its hinges, and a bunch of what appeared to be old municipal ledgers was scattered and rainsoaked outside the door. Inside was dim and suggestive of packing cases. I thought about going in. No way out. Once in there and confronted, I was trapped. Better to stay out here. Hit and run, sting like a wasp, run like a rabbit, or something.

It had gotten too dark now for me to see far. I couldn't spot any movement in the weeds. They'd have to get closer before I could see them. Or maybe they'd come along the road. Maybe I'd left tracks. These were city dudes. They wouldn't come loping along single file in the road, reading signs as they came. The tracks they knew horses ran on. But they'd come. And I was patient. I settled in a little tighter against the shed. It was corrugated metal and had once been painted white, but very little paint was left. There were remnants of milk cartons and wine bottles and beer cans and Devil Dog wrappers and other hints of civilized life having passed on. The whole area was an oasis of weeds and refuse in the middle of the city—cars, boats, people, lights, buildings, gestations, and high school kids were all around us, but in here, in the dark ten-acre wasteland—we could have been in a Sumatran rain forest. Hunting. It was getting colder and this close to the harbor the wind had picked up. I shivered a little. If the weather were better, it might have been more fun. Cops and robbers. Capture the flag. There was death involved, but that just made it serious; it didn't spoil the fun. Especially if death had very little sting left. And for me, it had barely any.

CHAPTER 32

They came out of the weeds, four abreast, spaced, looking carefully right and left. One of them, a tall fat man wearing a red warm-up jacket, carried the shotgun at port arms. The other three had handguns. The guy next to the shotgun carried a big silver flashlight. The kind that takes five D batteries. He was wearing a baseball cap and a brown plaid raincoat. Spiffy. He raised his hand and the four of them stopped. The guy with the flashlight talked with the guy carrying the shotgun. The other two gathered around them. Stupid. Easy to pick them all off, together like that. Except I had a gun that wasn't accurate that far, and only four bullets.

191

The group split up. Flashlight and Shotgun stayed put. The other two swung in a wide circle around the storage shack. I flattened on the ground. Nobody saw me, the circle they made was too big, trying, probably, to stay out of sight and range of the shack while the guy with the shotgun covered the front. I lost sight of the two circlers. I didn't like that. Then one of them whistled from behind the shack. The two guys in front began to move toward the open door. The big one had the shotgun leveled, his buddy turned on the flashlight and beamed it straight into the shack. I stayed flat. At the door they stopped. I couldn't see them either now. Then I heard someone clamber up into the building. One was in, one was out. No better time.

I came up into a crouch and slid around the corner of the building. Plaid Raincoat was standing on the ground, shining his big flashlight into the shack. Shotgun had gone in. I don't think he heard me. I had on jogging shoes and I was quiet. He must have sensed me coming and turned, bringing his right hand out of the doorway and turning the big automatic he held toward me. I shot him in the face and he went over and I was past him heading back into the weeds. As soon as I was in the weeds I hit the ground and as I did pellets whisked through the wet weeds above me, and the shotgun boomed. As it boomed I was back up and moving, heading to my right toward the river and the dam. I had to slow down. It was dark now and if I ran into a pile of girders or something, it would be a short misery before someone put me out of it. I began to feel my way along. The sound of them crashing through the weeds behind me had softened to a rustle. They must be doing the same thing. As I moved I stepped in something squishy. It was too dark to see what it was. I was glad. I could see headlights and taillights gleaming wetly from the Charles River Bridge. Misted by the rain and enhanced by the wet reflection they were elegant against the darkness. Not bad for a taillight. There was movement in front of me. I dropped to my knees. One of the bastards had gone around by the dirt road. The other two were still behind me. Or were there two in front? No, one would circle, two would chase. The movement continued while I strained into the dark to see him. Then he was there, a vague shape, a faint glint of light from the bridge touched the gun in his hand. Must have been stainless. Blued was better for this work. He was turned a little away from me. I fired at the middle of his body, he grunted and turned toward me. I fired again and he fired, his gun beginning to tilt up as he fell.

Right behind me there was the rush of running in the weeds and I snapped my last shot off toward it. Otherwise they'd be on me. The rush stopped, and I ran for the dam. Around the dam there was a landscaped area and atop the dam a building—in fact, two buildings that housed pumping equipment and offices and the harbor police. A rusty chain link fence maybe six feet high ran along the perimeter of the dam property and I had to go up and over it to get in. I put my gun back into its holster, grabbed hold of the top crossbar, and pulled myself up. I got a leg over, swung the other one up, and dropped on the dam side. The fence ought to be a real problem for the fat guy with the shotgun. He'd have to go around.

The wind was up now and I was on the run toward the locks. There were two locks, spanned by pedestrian walkways that swung open when a boat went through. They weren't big locks. There was no commercial traffic on the Charles. The locks were for pleasure boats. The dam was to keep the ocean from flowing upstream at high tide and leaving a layer of heavy salt water at the bottom of the river to kill all the bottom life.

There were streetlights on the dam property, lining the driveway entrance from City Square. I moved as fast as I could, staying low, trying not to silhouette against the street-lights. The wind was cold and I was soaked and shivering. I crossed a set of railroad tracks that breached the fence and ran across the dam compound and came to an end just short of the base of the Charlestown Bridge. If the fat guy with the shotgun knew about them, he wouldn't have to go around. If he knew about them and came out that way, I'd be a sitting duck in the lighted area with the choice of standing my ground with no gun or running for it across the two sets of locks on the narrow iron footpaths under the arc lights. In either case the guy with the shotgun could cut me in two while juggling two pickled eggs.

I stopped and moved back along the fence and crouched flat against it, next to the railroad tracks, beside the opening. The two gates were swung all the way back against the fence. A chain dangled from one of the gates, and a broken padlock was hooked through it. So much for security. I looked closer at the chain. It was merely looped through the fence link, the padlock still attached. Someone had cut it with a bolt cutter. God knows why. But vandalism marches to the beat of its own drummer. I took the chain out of the fence. Doubled, with the padlock end swinging free, it made a decent weapon. Not, on the whole, as decent as a shotgun, but better than an empty .38 with a two-inch barrel. The weeds grew right up to the outside of the fence, overgrowing the railroad tracks. On my side it was lawn and I felt the center of attention in the bare lawn with the streetlights shining twenty feet away, but they wouldn't see me until they got through the fence. If they came around, I could duck back through the gate into the weeds again. If they came one from each direction, I was probably going to be shot often.

They came on the railroad tracks. I saw the weed movement and then they were through the opening. First through was Shotgun, nearest me, and half a step behind Shotgun's left was a guy wearing aviator glasses and carrying a long-barreled revolver. I swung the chain down on the wrist that held the shotgun. The fat guy made a gasp, the shotgun fired upward and to the left and fell from his hand. I was shielded from the guy with the glasses by the fat man, who dropped to his knees, pressing his right hand against his chest and groping for the shotgun with his left. As the fat man dropped I hit his buddy across the face with my chain flail. His glasses broke and some of the glass got in his eyes. Blood appeared and he dropped the handgun and put both hands to his face. I shook the chain in a short circle to keep it out and away from him and then drove it down against the back of the fat man's neck. He had gotten the shotgun but was having trouble pumping a round up with his right hand numb and maybe broken. The second time the chain hit him he pitched forward and lay still on top of the gun, the barrel sticking out past his shoulder. His partner ran. With one hand still pressed against his right eye, he sprinted for the pedestrian walkway across the locks. I worried the shotgun out from under the fat man, pumped a round up. Shot the fat man as he lay, and went after his partner, working the pump lever as I ran. The partner was hurt and it slowed him. Pain will do that, even if it's pain elsewhere. The iron walkway zigzags across the locks. Over each lock it is actually on the dam doors that open and shut to let boats through and a sign says that the locks are subject to opening without warning.

By the time we were across the first lock I had closed the gap between us. The walkway was wet with rain and he had on leather-soled shoes. Blood ran down his face, he was running with one eye closed and his hand pressed against the eye. I was five feet behind him when we reached the second lock.

"Freeze," I said, "or I will blow the top half of you off."

He could tell from my voice that I was right

behind him. He stopped and put his left hand in the air. His right still pressed against his eye.

"My eye," he said. "There's something bad wrong with my eye."

"Turn around," I said.

He turned, his face was bloody. And the rain drenching down on it made the blood pink and somehow worse looking than if it had been just blood.

"I want you to go tell Mickey Paultz that you couldn't do it. That he sent five guys and it wasn't anywhere near enough. You hear me, scumbag? Tell him next time he better come himself."

"I'm going to lose my fucking eye," he said.

"I hope so," I said. "Now, be sure to tell Mickey what I said."

He stood silently, holding his eye, one hand looking silly sticking up in the air.

"Beat it," I said.

Still he stood, staring at me with one eye. I threw the shotgun in a soft spinning arc into the river. "Beat it," I said. "Or I will throw you in after it."

"My fucking eye," he said. And turned. And ran toward the Boston side.

I trailed after him at a more sedate pace, feeling the beginning fatigue of passion expended and a slowing of the adrenaline pump.

"You didn't kill her on me this time," I said aloud. "Not this time."

Beyond the locks was a parking lot, and beyond that North Station. I went around to the front of North Station and caught a cab back to Assembly Square. I looked like I'd been wrestling alligators and losing. The cabbie didn't appear to notice. A lot of North Station fares looked like that.

CHAPTER 33

Linda stood against the wall outside the pub at the Assembly Square Shopping Mall. She had dried out in the time she'd waited and her hair was curlier than usual where it had been rain-soaked. She stood motionless as I approached, and when she saw me her eyes widened but she made no other sign.

"How you doing, babe," I said. "You in town long?"

She stared at me and shook her head.

"Come here often?" I said.

"What happened?" she said, her voice soft.

"I thwarted them," I said.

Her soft voice was insistent and there was some color on her cheeks. It wasn't the flush of health, it was two red spots, unnatural and hot looking. "What happened, goddamn you?"

"There were five of them, I think I killed four. One I sent back to his boss with a message."

"You just killed four people? Just now? And then you come here and joke with me? 'You in town long?' Jesus Christ."

"They were trying to kill me."

"What was that stuff about losing me too," she said.

I felt very tired, it was hard to concentrate. "I don't know," I said. "What stuff?"

"You said you didn't want to lose me too. Were you talking about Susan?"

I remembered. I remembered other things. Feelings I'd had. I remembered on the locks in the dark rain with the wind off the harbor pulling my words away, *You didn't kill her on me this time.*

"I was thinking of a woman in Los Angeles," I said. "I let her get killed."

"Well, I'm not she," Linda said.

"I know. I'll call a cab and get us out of here."

"And then what?" Linda said.

"Cook a couple of steaks," I said. "Drink a little wine? Your place or mine?"

Linda shook her head. "Not tonight. I . . .

201

I can't tonight. I have never . . . I'm exhausted and I need to be alone and to think. I can't just eat and drink and . . . I can't do anything after something like this."

I nodded. "Okay," I said. "Let me get us home anyway."

I found a phone booth in the mall and called a cab, and Linda and I went and waited for it at the main mall entrance, inside, out of the rain. We didn't talk and Linda, normally the most touching of people, kept her hands buried in her pockets and stood a foot away.

The cab dropped us off at Linda's condo. I got out with her. She said, "I can go up all right alone. You better keep the cab."

"No," I said. "I want to see that you get home safely."

She shrugged and we went in. I stood beside her when she unlocked the door. She switched on the light. No one lurked within.

She put her hand on my chest and kissed me lightly on the mouth.

"Good night," she said. "I'm sorry, it's just . . . well, you should understand. I've never . . ."

"I know," I said. "I'll call you soon."

"Yes," she said. "I hope . . . I don't know. This was awful."

"I'm sorry," I said. "I'm sorry this part had to spill over. I'm sorry it had to splash on you."

"It's not your fault," Linda said. "But I'm sorry, too, that I had to see it, and to know this part of you."

"Part of the package," I said. "Part of the deal."

She nodded, her eyes still very wide and the pupils enormous. "You are a very fine man," she said. And closed the door.

CHAPTER 34

I got five hours sleep.

The doorbell rang at 7:30 in the morning, a steady ring, like someone had placed his thumb against it and leaned. I put on a bathrobe and pressed the buzz-in button for downstairs and opened my door and went to the kitchen. I put the water on to boil and got out the coffee and the coffee maker. I had the coffee measured into the pot when Belson came in my open apartment door. There was another cop with him that I didn't know.

I put three coffee cups on the counter.

"You look really adorable in the fucking robe, Chickie," Belson said.

"Either of you guys take cream or sugar?"

Belson shook his head. The other cop said, "Just black."

Belson said, "This is Carmine Lizotti."

I nodded at the cop. He said, "How ya doing?"

Belson said, "You wanna guess why we come by this morning?" He looked like he'd been up for some time. His thin face was clean shaven with the faint blue glow of a heavy beard under his tan. He had on a seersucker suit and a straw hat with a wide blue band, and his black loafers gleamed with polish. Lizotti was heavier and a little shorter with a wedge-shaped nose and a prominent chin. He had on a coarse weave summerweight blue blazer with his white shirt collar spread out over the lapels. He smoked a filter-tipped cigarette, holding the filter tip between his teeth when he talked.

"I'm guessing you found a 1980 Subaru hatchback with the left side torn off in the weed yard under Route 93 off City Square in Charlestown. And you checked the registration and found it was mine."

"Car's totaled," Lizotti said, his cigarette bobbing up and down in his teeth. "You oughta be driving an American car anyway."

"Serves me right," I said.

I poured the hot water over the coffee and

pressed the plunger down on the pot, squeezing the grounds to the bottom.

"French roast," I said. "That mean you won't drink it?"

"Subaru wasn't the only thing totaled in there," Belson said.

I got some cream out of the refrigerator, and a box of sugar out of the cupboard.

"Hope you don't require formal service," I said.

I put a couple of teaspoons on the counter near the cups.

"I got some whole wheat cinnamon and raisin bagels here," I said. "And some all natural cream cheese. No gum or other additives."

"Sure," Belson said. "We'd be fools not to."

Lizotti said, "For crissake, Frank, who is this guy, Julia fucking Child?"

"He's elegant, Liz. Everything just so. An elegant guy."

I put three bagels into the oven to heat, and took a block of cream cheese out of the refrigerator and unwrapped it and put it on a saucer. I got three butter knives out and put them beside the saucer.

"Got to let the coffee steep a little," I said. "And nobody likes a cold bagel."

"We found four fucking stiffs in there," Lizotti said.

"Three shot with a thirty-eight, one with a shotgun," I said.

"Probably," Belson said. "M.E. hasn't got a report yet."

I poured coffee into the three cups, and added some cream from the carton and sugar from the box. The box has one of those little metal fold-out pouring spouts. I stirred my coffee and sipped some.

"Water-decaffeinated," I said. "Mocha almond. You can get it at Bread and Circus in Cambridge."

Belson added sugar, no cream. Lizotti ignored his.

Lizotti said, "You admitting you did it?"

"Yep."

I put my coffee down, went to the bedroom, and got my gun. I brought it back into the kitchen, still in its clip-on holster, with the strap snapped. Lizotti's hand moved under his coat as I came back in. Belson shook his head.

"The weapon in question," I said, and gave it to Belson. He removed it from the holster, opened the cylinder, shook out the fresh load I'd put in before I went to bed, snapped shut the cylinder, and handed me back the holster and the five rounds. He dropped the gun in his coat pocket.

Lizotti said, "Been fired recently?"

I said, "Yes."

Lizotti said, "Give it a sniff, Frank."

Belson grinned at me and had a little more coffee.

"For crissake, Liz. The guy already confessed."

"The slugs you dig out of those guys will match the ones you test-fire from my gun," I said.

"How about the shotgun?" Lizotti said.

"It's in the river by the new locks," I said.

"It belonged to Fat Willie Vance," Belson said. "Spenser took it away from him and shot him with it."

I nodded.

Lizotti said to Belson, "How come you're so sure?"

"How I got to be sergeant," Belson said. "Intuition."

"That's who that was," I said. "It was kind of dark and I was rushed. I didn't even recognize him. Willie always uses a shotgun," I said to Lizotti.

"Used," Belson said.

"Yes."

"It was Willie's crew," Belson said. "I figure someone hired him to hit you, and they were overmatched. What I don't know is who."

"Quirk knows," I said.

Belson looked at Lizotti. "Okay," he said.

"Get dressed. We'll go downtown and talk with Marty and you'll give us a statement, in which you'll claim self-defense, and we'll see what we think."

I took the bagels out of the oven one at a time, juggling them to keep from burning my hands, and tossed them on the counter.

"Eat up," I said. "While I shower. Save me a bagel."

"You put four of them down by yourself?" Lizotti said.

"Yeah," I said. "Not bad for a guy who'd wear a maroon velour robe, huh?"

I showered and dressed and ate my bagel on the way downtown. Lizotti didn't join us in Quirk's office. Just Quirk, Belson, and little old *moi*. Three hours later I took a cab home, free for the moment, maybe forever, carless, but licensed still to pursue my trade. The cops had kept my gun, but I had another one. All in all it had worked out much better for me than it had for Fat Willie. As far as I knew it was his only shotgun.

CHAPTER 35

Sherry Spellman and I took the elevator down from Vince Haller's office and went out onto Staniford Street in the heat of August.

"Haller will help you in any way you need," I said.

She nodded.

"You understand the trust?"

She nodded.

"And that he's trust officer?"

"Yes."

"He'll help you with organization, with your tax situation. He'll help arrange credit until the trust starts to generate income."

"I understand," she said.

"And you can call me anytime." We turned left at Cambridge Street.

"I know," she said. She put her hand on my arm and stopped me. "I want to say thank you. But I want to say more than that and I don't know how."

I leaned over and kissed her on the forehead. "My pleasure," I said. "The next step is Tommy."

She stepped away and widened her eyes at me.

"I got into this thing because Tommy Banks asked me to find you. He's the only client I've had since we began. I think you two should talk."

"I don't know what to say to him."

"Maybe we can plan that out a little too. But you owe him the chance to talk."

"Yes," she said.

"Do you love him?" I said.

"Yes."

"Do you want to live with him again?"

"I don't know. I won't go back to dancing and all of that."

"What's 'all of that'?" I said.

"All of that discipline, that control, it . . . it submerges me. I am not just a dancer and Tommy a choreographer. I'm a puppet."

"So how could you be with him?"

"Maybe if he came with me."

"Join the church? Give up dancing?"

She frowned. "No," she said. "That wouldn't be fair. He could still be a dancer if I could be in my church."

"Any other men in your life?"

"There are men in the church I care about, but we never . . ."

I nodded. "Okay. Want to go to the studio?"

"Tommy's studio? No." She shook her head vigorously. "No."

"Okay," I said. "Neutral ground. My office."

She nodded. We walked down across the Common to my office. When we went in I looked automatically across the street at Linda's office. She was there but her back was to the window. I stared at her for a moment, feeling something very much like need tugging at my stomach. Then I sat down in my chair and called Tommy Banks.

He arrived a half hour later, his face tight, his movements constricted, like a man walking over a slippery spot on a winter street. Sherry stood when he came in. They looked silently at each other and then she stepped to him and kissed him lightly. He put his arms around her, but she stiffened and leaned her hips away from him. He knew it at once and took his arms away quickly. They stood back from each other, hurt showing in Banks's face.

"Same old passionate Sher," he said. It had

the sound of an ancient refrain. She shook her head slowly from side to side.

"Tommy," she said.

"You ready to come back," he said.

She looked at me. I remained silent.

"Tommy, I can't come back and be a dancer."

"God won't approve?" he said.

"Isn't there another way for us to be together?"

"You want me to move up in your fucking commune?" Tommy said. "Mumble beads all day or whatever you do?"

"That's not what we do," she said.

"Does it have to be either or?" I said. Having done such a swell job on my own love life, maybe I could start spreading it around.

"What do you mean?" Banks said.

"She does church work, you dance, but you share each other's evenings or whatever."

"She's a dancer," Banks said, "so am I. I won't let her throw her life away on some fucking superstition."

"It's my life, Tommy."

Banks turned toward her and his intensity trembled in the room.

"Your life is my life. I'm you and you're me. There's no my-life-your-life with us."

"Tommy," she said, and her voice was pressed and despairing, "I can't be with you

213

all the time. But we could be together some, often, but not always. I'm not a dancer anymore, Tommy. You can't choreograph me anymore."

Banks's breath was heaving. He opened his mouth and closed it and the tears began to run down his face. At his sides his hands clenched into white-knuckled fists.

"Separate people can still love," Sherry said.

"Them," Banks gasped. "Them or me."

"Don't," Sherry said. "Don't do that, Tommy."

They stood silently two feet apart. I felt the knot tighten inside me as I sat. I looked out my window. Linda wasn't there. I turned back, feeling a little sick.

"Them," Banks said as if he were spitting. He turned and walked out of the office, leaving the door open, and I heard his footsteps recede down the corridor. Sherry turned toward me and we looked at each other silently. She sat suddenly in my client chair and her body sagged and she put her face in her hands and cried. After a while I got up and went over and stood behind her and rubbed her shoulders a little and tried to think of something to say.

CHAPTER 36

I was at my apartment eating bean soup with
Paul when Susan called. Her voice was small.

"Hello," she said.

"Hello."

"How are you?"

"Still here," I said. "How about yourself?"

"I'm as far from you as I can get," she said.

"Not true," I said. "You could get a job in
Hong Kong."

"I don't mean it that way," she said. "I
mean I can't give you up. I can't altogether
leave you."

"Can you come back?"

"No."

"Getting any pressure from your guy friend?"

"Yes."

"He wants to move in?"

"Yes."

"You can't do that either."

"No," she said. I had never heard her voice so small, so wounded. For the first time since she left I felt her pain too.

"So you have two men in your life," I said, "and you can't give yourself completely to either one."

"Six years ago," she said, "on a beach on Cape Cod you asked me to marry you, and I said no. I said that you wouldn't fit in my world or me in yours and we were better as we were."

"I remember."

"That wasn't it," she said. "It was simply that I couldn't."

"And you still can't."

"Yes," she said. "I thought maybe it was just you, your intensity, your force. It has always scared me even when it attracted me."

"And . . ."

"But it's me too. I couldn't live with my husband. I can't live with my friend either."

"Even though you love him."

The line was quiet. "I love you too."

"When I came back from L.A.," I said, "I

216

had just failed more completely than I ever have. I betrayed you by making love to Candy Sloan. . . ."

"You had the right," Susan said. "That wasn't betrayal."

"Yeah, I told Candy that, too, but it was. I disapproved of me for it. And then I let them kill her."

"She got herself killed," Susan said.

"And I started getting scared that I wasn't everything. And I started needing you to make me complete, and that was when things started going to hell."

"I can't complete you," Susan said. "More important, you can't complete me. I have to do that myself."

"I know."

"Everything you've achieved you've achieved through strength, through force, through will. This you can't force. This you have to permit."

"It's your line of work," I said.

"Yes," Susan said. "Physician heal thyself, huh?"

I nodded.

Susan said, "Are you still there?"

"Yes."

"It will take a while," Susan said, "but we will resolve this."

"Yes."

Susan said, "I don't know how it will resolve, but I know this. I know in my bones that I love you, and that I cannot conceive of a life without you."

"Me too," I said.

"I will call you again soon," Susan said. Her voice was barely there.

"Yes," I said. "Good-bye."

"Good-bye."

I hung up.

Paul came into the living room and said, "Are you all right?"

"No, I'm not all right," I said. "But I won't die."

Paul's face was hard. "You've got to get off of this," he said. "If not for yourself, for me. You're losing Susan, I'm losing Susan and you."

"Goddamn it," I said, "you get as much as I have left. This is all there is of me now, there isn't any more. You won't lose me, but this is all you can fucking well have of me right now."

Paul's face was hurt and angry. "It's not selfishness," he said, "you've got to get off of Susan. There is a life ahead for you. Even if you don't lose her, you've got to get off of her. You are, for crissake, obsessive."

I felt my anger flare. And I looked at Paul's

determined face and saw that there were tears in his eyes.

"I'm sorry," I said. "I'm doing what I can. There will be more of me in a while. This thing will resolve."

Paul nodded.

"Now I have to go to work," I said.

"Don't be careless," Paul said.

"I won't be," I said. "I want to be around to see how this turns out."

CHAPTER 37

"It's like early congregationalism," Sherry said. We were sitting in the dining hall at the Middleton headquarters drinking coffee at a table where the morning yellow sun made a pleasing yellow splash on the space between us. "We meet once a week on Tuesday evenings right here and decide on church business. I'm council chairman."

There were two or three kitchen workers gearing up for lunch, but otherwise there was no one else in the room. My new approach to cutting back on coffee was to drink it with a lot of milk and sugar. After a while it would be easy to wean myself altogether, more milk and less coffee each time, and eventually I'd have it done. The coffee mugs were the old thick white china ones they used to use in diners. I got up and went to a coffee urn and refilled mine, added a lot of milk and some sugar, and went back to the table. The smell of stew and coffee enriched the room.

"And the money?"

"The money is being handled by the trust department at Mr. Hallers's bank and they issue us a check for the interest every month. They said it would be about two thousand a month."

"That be enough?"

"I think so. We are quite self-sufficient and we are going to work on that. This compound is paid for. We raise most of our vegetables and eggs. We're going to preserve fruits and vegetables this year. We can't give people a stipend really, anymore, but they can supplement by working outside and we're considering how to make money."

Sherry had filled out a little. She had a lot of color from working outdoors, and she seemed firmer to me.

"What about Reverend Winston?" she said.

"He's agreed to supply evidence against Paultz," I said. "When the warrants are all in place they will bust Mickey and indict him and Winston will testify and they'll put Paultz away."

"What will happen to him?" Sherry said.

"Winston? I suspect he'll get a suspended sentence, and then maybe they'll give him a new identity and he'll disappear in some witness protection program."

"Because Mickey Paultz will try to have him killed?"

"Yes. We've got Winston covered now so Paultz can't get at him. And Paultz thinks he's bought silence with the church donation. But when Winston testifies . . ."

Sherry nodded. She was resting her chin on her clenched right fist and I was struck by the bizarre conjunction of Mickey Paultz and this religious little kid.

"I hope he'll be all right," Sherry said. "Where is he?"

"He's covered," I said.

"Do you know anything about Tommy?" she said.

I shook my head. "Paul says he's canceled rehearsals and they are a week and a half away from a performance."

"My God," she said.

"Not his style?"

"Oh, Lord, no. Nothing came before performance. Nothing."

The sunlight had moved slightly and now touched her hands where they lay motionless beside her coffee cup on the table. The brightness made her skin seem faintly translucent. And her unadorned hands seemed very vulnerable.

"I hope he hasn't done anything to himself," she said. She was studying the sunlight on her hands.

"Most people don't," I said.

"Would you find out if he's all right?" she said.

She had pulled her hair back from her face and caught it with some kind of pin at the nape of her neck. She wore no makeup. Her face as she looked at me seemed almost devoid of experience, as if it had begun just this morning. Her eyes were very pale blue.

"Sure," I said. "I'll take a look."

"We . . . I can't pay you."

"What are friends for," I said.

She reached one of her hands toward me through the splash of sun and took my hand. And held it.

"You are a friend," she said. "I didn't know there were people like you. I've never met anyone like you."

"I am a dandy," I said.

She reached her other hand across and patted the top of my hand.

"Yes," she said. "You are. You do what you say you'll do. You care about people. You aren't mean. You're strong. You're a very wonderful man."

"And I have a winsome smile," I said. "Don't forget that."

She kept patting my hand. "I pray for you each day," she said.

"It can't hurt," I said.

CHAPTER 38

Looking for Tommy Banks didn't seem too complicated. I'd check his apartment and if he wasn't there I'd check the dance studio, and if he wasn't there I'd think about it. My heart wasn't in it. But if the rigid little bastard had in fact killed himself, Sherry was going to pull the guilt of it right up over her ears.

The phone rang. I answered. It was Devane, the statie.

"Somebody blew Mickey Paultz away," he said.

"Who?"

"Don't know."

"Why?"

"Same answer. He was sitting in his car on

the third floor of the parking garage at Quincy Market. Somebody put two bullets in his head from the passenger side, probably sitting next to him. Twenty-two-automatic shell casings were on the car floor. And that's all there is."

"A nice guy like that," I said. "Doesn't seem fair, does it?"

"Seems like you went to a lot of trouble to rig something that isn't going to happen."

Alone in my office I shrugged. "I got Winston out of the church," I said.

"And Broz has the heroin trade now, either way," Devane said.

"So who would scrag poor old Mickey?"

"Hell," Devane said. "Who wouldn't?"

"Anyway, it takes the heat off Winston," I said. "They still going to prosecute him?"

"I don't know," Devane said. "My guess is no. All they've got him for is laundering some money and I figure Rita's got better things to do than spend a week in court getting some guy two years suspended and a thousand-dollar fine."

"You mean a miscreant will be walking the streets of this commonwealth unpunished?" I said.

"I think so," Devane said, and hung up. I got up and went out of my office to check on Tommy Banks.

He wasn't in his apartment, and he wasn't at the studio, so I went back to my office. He wasn't there either. In fact, wherever I went for the rest of the day, Tommy Banks wasn't there. Where was Mr. Keen when I really needed him. I checked with Belson at Homicide. No unidentified bodies that resembled Banks had turned up.

Unrequited-love suicides usually wanted people to know they'd done it. It was a way to say, *See what you've done to me, you bitch.* So the fact that no one had found his body was a good sign. I wasn't sure I wanted to explain it to Sherry just that way. I called Sherry at 5:15 to tell her that as far as I could tell, Tommy Banks had not done himself in, and was probably off somewhere sulking. She thanked me. She said if I heard anything, I should let her know. I said I would, and hung up. No wasted conversation. Efficient, neat, economical of movement and gesture. And without a goddamned clue to where Tommy Banks was or where he would be. Some days I thought it might be better to be sloppy and successful. Maybe I should practice dogged determination. I stood and walked over to the window and looked down on Berkeley Street. Spot him from the air. No luck. The late afternoon commuter crowd was moving into the subway kiosk below me. Across the street Linda's office was empty. I called her office. She had left for the day. I called her home. No answer. I hung up and sat in my chair and clasped my hands behind my head and put my feet up. So it would be a quiet evening. Paige was up visiting Paul and they were going to a concert. Linda had left for the day. Susan was on the West Coast with a guy friend. That was the bad news. The good news was it would give me lots of time to think about Mickey Paultz getting wasted. I looked at my watch, 5:24. I thought about someone shooting Mickey Paultz in the head with a .22-caliber automatic at close range. I tried to wonder why. I tried to care. I looked at it from every angle I could conceive. And finally I gave it up. I looked at my watch again, 5:27. I looked at the phone. It didn't say anything. I looked out the window some more. People were still heading into the subway. Nobody looked up at my office. Nobody called. Nobody came in. I thought about going over to the Harbor Health Club and working out. I thought about going down to the Quincy Market and buying some finger food and walking around looking at tourists. I got my bottle of Old Bushmill out of my desk and had a small snort from the bottle. Decisive. Not a man to sit around and do nothing. I had another small tap from the bottle neck.

I hadn't seen Linda Thomas since the shootout in the weeds. Broad had no sense of adventure. She'd liked Darth Vader okay. What was wrong with me.

I had some more whiskey.

Nice date. *We'll go to the movies and after, I'll shoot four guys.* Linda probably wanted to get a snack afterward. No imagination. Sit around, eat and drink. Get logy. Probably take in too much salt and saturated fats. Movies and a shootout, now that was different. If you skipped butter on the popcorn, it was cholesterol-free, non-fattening, and low sodium.

I drank some more, and swiveled around and put my feet up on the windowsill, and watched the sky get slowly dark over Linda's empty building.

CHAPTER 39

I found Tommy Banks through a combination of luck and good detective work. The luck part was that I was in my office thinking about coffee when Banks walked in the door. The good detective work involved saying, "Ah-ha, Tommy Banks."

He looked awful. He was hollow-eyed and gray-faced and there wasn't much verve in his step. There was about him a kind of exhausted rigidity that kept him unlimber, but slow, as he moved.

"She's still seeing that fucker Winston," he said.

I knew who "she" was. I did the same thing.

When I said "she" it was always Susan. When he said it he meant Sherry.

"I've been looking for you," I said.

"Me? What for?"

"She asked me to," I said.

He shook his head. "Shit," he said. "She's worried what I'd find out."

"Yeah?" I nodded toward my guest chair.

"Yeah." He sat.

"Why shouldn't she see Winston?" I said. "There's probably stuff he knows about running the church that she needs help with."

"She don't need to stay all night," Banks said.

I raised my eyebrows. It was what I did when I didn't know what to say. This summer they'd been up a lot.

"Did she?" Banks was insistent that I respond. He leaned stiffly toward me. "Did she?"

"No," I said. "I wouldn't think she'd have to stay all night."

"Now do you believe me?" Banks said.

"Believe you about what," I said.

"That something's going on there. That there's been something going on for a long time and they're fooling all of you."

"Tommy," I said. "The woman you love is sleeping with another guy, maybe. That's aw-

231

ful for you. But it happens. It's not something I can prevent."

"They're doing something," Banks said. "They been doing something since I first talked to you and you never found it out. You think she's a little gingham sweetie that likes to pray. That's not her. She's been jerking you around just like she did me."

"What do you think they're doing," I said.

"I don't know, but she is not a Holy Roller. I know her. I know her better than anyone. That's why at first I figured they'd kidnapped her. She wouldn't go Jesus freak on her own."

"That's why you made up the kidnap stuff?"

"Yeah, I figured it was true but I figured you wouldn't look all that hard for her if I just said I thought so."

"And you still don't think she's there 'cause she wants to be?"

"She wants to be there okay. Like she wants to fuck Winston. But not for God."

"Love?" I said.

He shrugged. "I don't know how much she's willing to sacrifice for love. I never saw much sign of it."

"So you think there's something else."

"Smart," Banks said. "You are really smart."

I sighed.

"But you don't know what the something else is," I said.

"Aren't you supposed to be able to find out stuff like that?"

I felt tired. I thought about coffee, maybe add a little Bushmill to it, an ethnic pick-me-up. I didn't want to work on this case anymore. I was tired of Banks, and of his obsession, and of Sherry and Winston and the Reorganized Church. I was tired of me too.

"Yeah," I said. "I'm supposed to find out stuff like that. It's just that I thought I already had."

"You found out shit," Banks said.

"I find a lot of that," I said.

Banks looked like he might break. He radiated tenseness and hurt.

"You been following her," I said.

He nodded.

"And she went to Winston's and didn't come out all night."

He nodded again.

"You watched all night."

"Yes."

I swung my chair around toward my window and stood up and looked out. The sun reflected off Linda's window and I couldn't see if she was there or not. The sun coming in my window was hot and there was a wind off the river. I could see the pedestrians lean slightly into it as they walked. The summer skirts on the women were pressed between

233

their legs and people with hats kept a hand on them. An empty paper cup with golden arches on it skittered along the gutter up Berkeley Street toward police headquarters. I envied it. It had direction.

I turned back to Banks.

"I'll look into it," I said.

"You took all my money last time and found shit," Banks said. "You cleaned me out."

"No charge, this time," I said. "You're still under warranty."

CHAPTER 40

Martin Quirk met me after work at Harvard Gardens for a couple of beers. From the way he looked you wouldn't know if he was finishing the day or starting. His short black hair was perfectly in place. His white shirt was full of starch. He came into the bar the way cops do, like it was his bar, in his city. Despite the name, Harvard Gardens was a neighborhood bar in Boston and better than most. It was across from Mass General Hospital and the parking lot for the Charles Street Jail. The mix of nurses, interns, jail guards, and people from Beacon Hill made for a nice texture. And if you wanted, you could eat. I didn't want to eat. I was sipping Irish whiskey and chasing it with beer. Quirk had the same.

"How are you," he said.

"I'm as restless as a willow in a windstorm," I said.

"You in touch with Susan at all?" Quirk said. He took a delicate sip of Irish whiskey and swallowed and put the whiskey glass down and drank some beer. His hands were thick. He was very exact in his movements.

"Yes," I said. "We talk on the phone."

"Give her my love," Quirk said.

I nodded.

Quirk drank again, he extended the little finger slightly as he sipped the whiskey.

"You want to know about Mickey, right?"

"How did you know?" I said.

"You want to know about everything you've had anything to do with in the last ten years," Quirk said.

"And I adore hearing you talk," I said. "Your voice is so musical."

"You talk with Devane?" Quirk said.

"Yes. He told me Mickey was shot sitting in his car in the Quincy Market parking garage. He said whoever shot him probably was sitting beside him. The murder weapon was a twenty-two automatic, and the brass was on the floor of the car."

Quirk smiled and sipped another very small

sip of whiskey. "Hell," he said, "you know what I know."

"Nothing else?" I said.

Quirk shook his head.

"How about speculation."

"It had to be someone Mickey wasn't scared of," Quirk said. "No bodyguards. Mickey didn't usually travel without back-up."

"Unless the back-up was who did it."

"But why would they do it there, with a twenty-two automatic?"

"Twenty-twos are chic these days," I said. "Like flavored popcorn."

Quirk shrugged.

"We're assuming it had something to do with the drug business. And the deal you and Devane rigged to put him away might have triggered something."

"Broz?" I said.

"I don't think so," Quirk said.

"No," I said. "I don't either. Joe went to some trouble so he wouldn't have to waste Mickey. Why would he do that and then when it was set have Mickey buzzed?"

Quirk signaled to a waitress for two more beers. "So who would want Mickey dead?" Quirk said.

"His supplier," I said.

"For fear Mickey would rat on him," Quirk

said. "But how would the supplier know we were going to bust Mickey?"

The waitress brought two drafts and left.

Quirk and I were looking at each other.

"Could be a leak inside," Quirk said. "Of course it may just be something we don't know anything about. A jealous girlfriend, a mob deal that hasn't surfaced."

I nodded. "But," I said, "if you assume that, it gives you nothing to think about and nowhere to go."

"That's right," Quirk said. "So maybe somebody knew that Mickey was going to fall, and figured he'd talk out of turn."

I nodded. "So they got him to meet them alone in the parking garage and killed him."

"It had to be someone who had reason to meet him alone, and someone he wasn't afraid of."

"And someone who would use a twenty-two automatic," I said.

Quirk nodded. He was looking at the half empty shot glass in front of him. He put a forefinger into the whiskey and took it out and put it into his mouth and sucked on it absently.

"A broad," he said.

"Fills the criteria," I said.

"Say it is the supplier," Quirk said. "Is she part of the deal or do they hire someone?"

"Even a woman," I said. "Unless he knew her or something, Mickey wouldn't go without a couple of sluggos, even if it was a woman." I finished my whiskey and drank some beer. "Do we call her a hit person?" I said.

"A gunette," Quirk said.

"So we figure that a woman Mickey knows gets him to meet her in the Quincy Market parking garage. Or to meet her somewhere else and drive there. . . ."

"Meet her and drive there," Quirk said. "If it's full, she goes someplace else."

"Right," I said, "so he meets her someplace. They go to the garage. He parks and she blasts him."

Quirk nodded.

"Then she gets out of the car, walks over to the stairs, and down and out and . . ." I shrugged.

"Yeah," Quirk said, and shrugged a replica of my shrug. "And there we are. You got anything to add? What made you so interested?"

I told him what Tommy Banks had said about Sherry Spellman and Bullard Winston.

"That's not much," Quirk said.

"I know, but Mickey was all there was. It was the only thing that didn't make sense. The only event that didn't fit into the explanation."

Quirk nodded. "Yeah, I know. You don't have any handle on the kid and Winston, so you start at the other end and see if it leads backwards to them."

"Back door," I said.

"You think this Spellman kid could shoot Mickey Paultz to death?"

"No," I said.

"But you could be wrong," Quirk said.

"I surely could," I said. "I'm getting used to it. But the kid?" I shook my head. " 'Course I would have said she'd never spend the night with Winston either."

"Svengali?" Quirk said.

"Christ, I don't know."

"Maybe he used her to get Mickey."

"He wouldn't need to," I said. "He and Mickey were in cahoots."

"But Mickey knew you had Winston's confession," Quirk said. "Winston was hiding from him. If Winston set up a meeting, Mickey would have brought troops."

"What if Winston said no troops, as a condition. And Mickey thought, okay, I'll meet him and do it myself, only Winston beat him to it," I said. "Mickey have a piece?"

Quirk shook his head. I said, "Okay, maybe a variation on that."

"So where's the girl come in?" Quirk said.

"Maybe she doesn't."

240

Quirk finished his whiskey. "You got a handful of broken parts," he said. "Nothing fits."

"But I have a nice personality," I said.

Quirk snorted. "What I'd do," he said, "if I were you, is I'd go talk with Broz, or at least Vinnie Morris. Mickey's supplier needs an outlet now that Mickey's dead, and Joe was all set up for it anyway."

I nodded.

"I'd do it myself," Quirk said. "But they hate talking business with me."

I nodded again. "I been thinking about the back-door approach."

Quirk raised his eyebrows slightly.

"What if I had everything backward," I said. "What if Mickey wasn't running Winston. What if Winston was running Mickey?"

Quirk pointed his chin up and put his head back and stretched his neck and sucked on his front teeth a little.

"I'll have to think about that," he said.

"Me too," I said.

"Yeah," Quirk said, "but for you it's harder."

CHAPTER 41

My living room was littered with records and Paul and Paige were lying among them listening to Anita Ellis and Ellis Larkins. It was an album Paul had bought me as a half joking Father's Day gift. They were drinking jug wine and smoking. I sniffed.

"I believe I sense the presence in this room of a controlled substance," I said.

"You going to shoot at us?" Paige said.

"With the price of bullets the way it is," I said, "I'll let you off with a vicious beating."

Paige grinned at me. "Oooh, good," she said. "I'm really into that."

I went to the refrigerator and got a beer and sat at the counter and sipped it and thought and listened to Anita Ellis and thought. Paul and Paige passed the joint back and forth between them and the smell of marijuana grew richer. *Back door.* The Anita Ellis album ended and Paul put on a group called Razmatazz. *What if Winston were running Paultz?*

"They sound like halfway between Manhattan Transfer and the Four Freshmen," Paige said.

"Except the Freshmen had no female vocalist," Paul said.

Winston had churches around the country, disciples to mule the stuff around, a built-in way to launder the money. *What if Mickey Paultz worked for Winston? Then what?* I got another beer and a shot and went back to the counter. *Then everything was possible.*

Paige was lying on her back with her head in Paul's lap.

"Lemme look at the album cover," she said.

If Winston were the big boss, then he'd conned us all. When I started nosing about, he'd tried threatening me off. Then he'd had Paultz send his bozos to threaten me. And then when that didn't work he'd conned me, and everyone else. He'd set Paultz up and while he was doing that he'd arranged a new retail outlet for himself, then he killed Paultz before Paultz got wise, and once everything

243

died down he'd go back to work. Except he was no longer head of the church.

"But Sherry is."

Paul said, "What?"

Paige mimicked him. "Whaaat?"

They both giggled.

"Thinking out loud," I said.

I looked at my watch, it was 9:15. I looked at the two kids lying on the floor together listening to music, smoking some grass, and drinking some wine, and giggling at things that grass made funny. If Sherry were in love with Winston, maybe she would do what he asked. Maybe she'd cover for him. Maybe a kid full of God and need would give her lover Christian forgiveness and help him in the heroin trade. And it should work. Hell, I'd even extorted some capital from Mickey Paultz for them to use while they lay low. No wonder she liked me. A friend in need is a friend indeed. I shook my head. The possibilities buzzed around inside my skull. There was not a single piece of evidence to make me think all these things. It was entire speculation rooted only in the fact that Tommy Banks had seen Sherry spend the night with Winston or he said he'd seen it. Tommy had lied to me before. Most people had. Susan too. I poured a little more whiskey. I drank some and chased it with beer. There was no more beer in the bottle. I

244

got another bottle. I didn't know a fact. I didn't know who was with whom or who was in charge of what or who was good and who was bad and what to do. Maybe I should forget about it and lecture the kids on drug abuse. I tried saying *drug abuse* and slurred the *s*, and decided to forgo the lecture.

Paige raised her head from Paul's lap and put her arms around his neck and pulled him forward toward her. I drank most of the shot of whiskey. What I should do is sleep on it. I should just finish off the beer I was drinking and then go to bed and sleep on the situation and no doubt would wake up knowing just what I should do. That was it. I'd sleep on it. I tried saying *sleep* and slurred the *s*. So I went to bed.

CHAPTER 42

I woke up the next morning knowing exactly what I had to do. And I did it. I got out of bed and took two aspirin. Then I went into the kitchen. Paul and Paige had opened the sofa bed in the living room and were asleep in a tangle of bedclothes. Not neat sleepers. I made coffee and sat at the counter and drank it. I turned on the CBS morning news so I could watch Diane Sawyer. Maybe I should write her a letter. If it didn't work out with Susan, or Linda . . . I raised my coffee cup to her. "Music beyond a distant hill," I said. Diane ignored me. The phone rang. It was only 7:15. Too early for Susan to be calling from San Francisco. Maybe Diane Sawyer.

I said, "Hello."

It was Hawk. He said, "You want to rescue what's left of your body 'fore it's too late?"

"You just getting in?" I said.

"No way, babe. Something in the genes, got to git up and git to choppin' that old cotton."

"And lifting that barge," I said, "and toting that bale."

"And beating my feet on de Mississippi mud."

I said, "You want to run?"

"Yeah, I want to pump some iron too. You busy?"

"No," I said. "There's things I should do but I don't know what they are or how I should find out."

"You ought to be used to that," Hawk said. "I be by."

I took a shower and put on sweat clothes and went down to the street. Hawk's Jaguar pulled into the curb as I came out. He left it there on a crosswalk and we set out along the river.

"Want to go long," Hawk said. "You look like you got stuff to sweat out."

I nodded. We made the big circle, up along the Charles to the Western Avenue Bridge, then across the river and down the Cambridge side along Memorial Drive to the Charles River Dam and back up along the esplanade to my apartment. It took us a little more than an hour. But when we got back I was loose and sweat-soaked and the hangover had gone.

"Lemme get a change of clothes," I said, "and we'll go over to the health club."

Upstairs I put jeans and loafers and a clean shirt into my gym bag, along with a gun. The shower was running. And Paige was alone in the sofa bed with a long exposure of naked thigh sticking out from under the covers. Hawk came out of my kitchen with a glass of orange juice and pulled the spread over her. She stirred but didn't wake up. I got some orange juice too and was drinking it when Paul came out of the shower wearing a towel.

Hawk said, "You looking pretty good for a fag dancer."

Paul said, "A fag dago dancer."

Hawk nodded and grinned and put a hand out and Paul gave him a low five.

"Sherry Spellman called you," Paul said to me. "And said for you to call her as soon as you got in. I wrote the number on the edge of the *Globe* there. It looks like Tommy's studio number. She said be sure and call, it's very important."

He went into the living room and began to rummage in his dance bag. I called Sherry.

Sherry answered on the first ring.

"We're all here at Tommy's studio," she said. "Tommy wants you here too."

"Who's *we all*," I said.

There was a sound of mild confusion at the other end of the phone and then Banks's voice replaced Sherry's.

"I got Winston and her," he said. "You get over here and they'll tell you what's been going on. You bring any cops and I'll kill them both."

"Fifteen minutes," I said.

"No cops," Banks said, and hung up.

I put on a warm-up jacket and took my gun out of the gym bag. I put the gun in the right-hand pocket of the warm-up jacket and said to Hawk, "Banks has Winston and Sherry Spellman as hostages. You want to come along?"

Hawk grinned happily. "Sure."

We went in Hawk's Jaguar. As he drove he unlocked the glove compartment and took out a 9-millimeter automatic and put it in his lap.

"You could tuck it in your jock," I said.

"No room," Hawk said. "You want to tell me who to shoot?"

"Christ," I said, "I don't know. Everybody but me, I think."

Hawk went straight up Commonwealth and turned left onto Mass Ave. I told him my speculations on Sherry and Winston and the heroin business.

Hawk pulled the Jag up along the curb in front of Symphony Hall. Tommy's studio was around the corner.

"Banks is expecting me," I said. "If he sees you, he may panic."

Hawk said, "I wait till you go on in and then I'll drift along up and hang around outside the door, see if I can hear what's happening. It don't sound good, I come in."

"What wouldn't sound good," I said. "You think I need back-up for a middle-aged chore-ographer?"

Hawk shrugged. "You ain't right yet, babe, you still ain't all you was."

"Okay," I said, "just remember I don't know who the good guys are yet."

"Maybe there ain't any," Hawk said.

"Maybe there never will be," I said, and got out of the Jag.

Hawk got out of his side and leaned his fore-arms on the roof and watched me walk to-ward the corner.

"You learning," he said.

I turned the corner.

CHAPTER 43

Sherry was standing beside Bullard Winston against the mirrored wall on the far side of the dance studio away from the windows. Tommy Banks leaned his back against one of the Lally columns that split the room. He held a nondescript .38 police special in his right hand. When I came in he pointed it briefly toward me then back toward Sherry and Winston and then, indecisively, at a point more or less in between us. I moved away from the door. If Hawk came in quickly, I didn't want to be in his way. I was careful to move toward the windows, away from Sherry and Winston, so that Banks wouldn't be able to point the gun at all of us together. Banks understood. He went straight to Sherry and took her arm and held her in front of him. He pointed the gun at Winston.

"I caught them together again," he said. "I stayed on them and I caught them together."

"Painful," I said. "But not illegal." I stayed away from them. It meant Tommy would have to talk a little louder and Hawk would hear better from the hall.

"Look on that table," Banks said.

There was a canvas mail sack on the table where the coffee machine stood.

"Look in the bag," Banks said.

The bag was full of Baggies and the Baggies, neatly tied with green twistems, contained something that looked like heroin. It also looked like milk sugar but most people didn't bag and transport milk sugar.

"The stuff that dreams are made of," I said.

"They had it," Banks said. "They had that stuff with them."

"That's not legal," I said.

Banks jabbed the gun toward Winston.

"Tell him what you're doing," Banks said.

"You're sick," Winston said. "You're sick with jealousy."

Winston looked at me.

"Yes, Sherry and I love each other. And I'm sorry that this man has to be hurt. But love does what it will. You know that, Spenser."

"Bullshit," Banks said. His voice hissed out, scraping over his pain. "She doesn't love you. Get her away from you and she'll recover. You're the one that's sick and you made her sick."

Sherry stood very still. Her eyes were wide and her face very small at the motionless center of the storm.

Winston shook his head. He seemed sad.

"Tommy," he said. "You can't do this. You can't plant this dope or whatever it is on us and hold us prisoner and try to claim we're guilty of something."

Banks put the gun to Sherry's head, pressing the muzzle against her temple.

"Truth," he hissed. "Tell him the truth or I'll kill her."

Winston looked even sadder. "Tommy," he said. "Tommy, don't."

Banks pressed the gun harder against Sherry's temple. She winced. "Tommy," she said. Her voice was frightened. I eased my hand up toward my jacket pocket.

"Tell him." Tommy's voice was barely human.

"It's the truth," Winston said. "So help me God, I have told the truth."

Banks thumbed the hammer back, I put my hand into my jacket pocket.

"He's lying," Sherry said, and her voice was

a soft scream. "He made me help him. He has been dealing drugs for years."

"Paultz worked for him," I said.

"Yes. And when you forced him out, he made me work with him. He drugged me, he . . . he has power."

"You vicious little lying bitch," Winston said. There was something that looked like genuine horror in his face. Banks turned the gun toward him. "She's lying," Winston said. "She's lying. Yes, all right, I helped her. Yes, we were running heroin. But she was the one. It was her operation. I fronted for her."

Sherry said, "Kill him, Tommy, don't let him say those things. He's made me do awful things. Kill him, kill both of them and we'll go away."

I said, "Tommy."

Winston said, "See, she'll use anyone." His voice was up three octaves, it seemed, and it squeaked with terror and rage and franticness. "Don't let her use you. Don't do it for her, Banks. She's . . ." He groped for words. "She's satanic. She's . . ."

Banks shot him. Twice. It was a mistake. He should have shot me first. Sherry wrenched away from him and my bullet hit Tommy in the middle of the chest, and he fell over on his back and lay perfectly still. Winston was on the floor too. He had lurched back against the mirrors and left a long smear of blood on the mirrors as he slid to the floor. Both men were dead. You see enough of it, you know. I put my gun back into my jacket pocket. Sherry went to her knees beside Banks and as I walked toward her she picked up his gun and aimed it at me, holding it in both hands. Her face was puckered and intense. Like a school-child doing math.

I said, "Sherry. It's okay. It's over."

"Yes, it is, you motherfucker," she said. Her face still concentrated. "For you it's over."

"Winston was right," I said.

"I'm right," she said. "I'm the only one that knows."

"You wanted me to look for Tommy so you'd know what he was up to."

She smiled at me without losing her intensity.

"You simple tool," she said. "I've used you for anything I wanted to use you for and now I'm going to kill you and take all my money and go away."

"You killed Mickey," I said.

"Of course."

I began to walk toward her.

"Stay," she said.

I kept coming.

"I'm going to kill you," she said.

"So what," I said.

She fired and the slug hit me in the right side of the chest. Everything slowed down. I could feel myself rock back and then right myself and take another step. I watched her finger tighten on the trigger, watched the cylinder begin to rotate counterclockwise, saw the hammer rise and fall and saw the muzzle flash and felt another thump, lower on the right side, still. I could feel my life begin to slither out of me. The hammer started back again when I reached down and grasped the gun by the barrel and slowly pulled it away from her with my left hand. I took hold of her throat with my right and began to raise her from her knees. She was far away from me now, way out at the very end of my extended arm, the hand at the end of that arm tightening with infinite patience on her throat. There was a remote sound and Hawk glided into the room and took her away from my hand and bent liquidly over me. The light in the room was very clear and still. I was greatly distant from it now and everything looked as if it were being viewed at the bottom of a clear lake. Hawk leaned over me. I realized I was on the floor. He pressed his mouth against mine. And breathed. As he breathed he tore away my shirt. He'd be looking for the wound, and when he found it he'd need a compress of some kind. I wondered if it would work. Just curiosity. It didn't matter much. I couldn't see what he was doing anymore. I had slithered out entirely.

CHAPTER 44

The lake was still and crystalline as I crossed it, and then became part of it so that the infinite clarity seemed to radiate from me and I could taste the brilliant stillness. Ahead was darkness. As I moved into it I noticed that there was scrub growth in parts of the oil field. When I was very close I could see them and see how the wind made their shapes contort as their branches moved restively, like animals too long restrained. Then I heard the shots. The sound sat on top of the wind the way a bird sits on a power line. I whirled, looking for a muzzle flash, and spotted some over to my left as more shots rode in on the wind. I ran toward them, my gun out. Two more shots. I banged into the superstructure of one of the pumps and spun around and staggered and kept my feet and kept going toward the spot where the memory of muzzle flash still vibrated in my mind. There was a brief flare of what must have been headlights swinging away, and then only the wind sound and the darkness. The wind had cooled, and there was thunder rolling to the west, and a new smell of rain in the air. I stopped for a moment and listened, staring toward the place where I'd seen the muzzle flashes and the headlights. Then lightning made a jagged flash, and I saw a car parked ahead of me. I moved toward it. I reached the car before the thunder caught up to the lightning.

The car was a five-year-old Plymouth Duster. It was empty. I listened and heard nothing but the wind. The lightning flashed again. In front of the car was a wide, cleared space, maybe for parking. I saw no people. The rain smell was stronger now, and the thunder came closer upon the lightning. The storm was moving fast. I opened the car door and reached in and, crouched behind the open door, I turned on the headlights.

Nothing happened. Nothing moved. I went flat on the ground, it was gravel, and looked underneath the car. Nothing. I got up carefully and moved out from the car in a crouch.

The headlights made a wide theatrical swash of visibility in the darkness. Twenty feet in front of the car was Franco Montenegro's body and next to him was Candy's.

I went down on my knees beside her, but she was dead, and I knew it even before I felt for a pulse and couldn't find it. She had taken a couple of bullets in the body. There was blood all over her front. Beside her on the ground her purse was open. The .32 was out. Unfired. She'd tried. Like I'd told her to. There was a small neat hole in her forehead from which a small trickle of dark blood traced across her forehead. I glanced at Franco. He had a similar hole. The last two shots I'd heard. The coup de grâce, one for each. I sat back on my heels and stared at Candy. Despite the blood and the bullet hole she looked like she had. For something as large as it is, death doesn't look like much at first.

The lightning and the thunder were nearly simultaneous now, and small spatters of rain mixed with the wind. I looked at Franco. Near his right hand was a gun. I moved over and, without touching the gun, lowered myself in a kind of push-up and smelled the muzzle. No smell of gunfire. He lay on his stomach, his face turned to one side. Blood soaked the back of his shirt. With my jaw clamped tight I rolled him over. There was no blood in front. The bullet hadn't gone through. He'd been shot from behind. Candy had been shot from in front. I got up and walked maybe fifteen feet back from Franco's body. On the soft gravel of the parking area were bright brass casings. The shooter had used an automatic, probably a 9-millimeter. I walked back and looked down at Candy. The rain was beginning to fall steadily, slanted by the wind. Already some of the blood was turning pink with dilution.

I looked around the parking area. There was nothing to see. I looked at Candy again. There was nothing more to see there either. Still, I looked at her. The rain was hard now, and dense, washing down on her upturned face. The wind was warm no longer. Candy didn't care. My clothing was soaked, my hair plastered flat against my skull. Rain running off my forehead blurred my vision. Candy's mascara had run, streaking her face. I stared down as the rain washed it away too.

"Some bodyguard," I said.

We were quiet. The band on the roof was playing "Indian Summer." The smell of flowers seemed to have faded. The smell of Candy's perfume was stronger. My mouth was dry.

"Is dancing too systematic for you?" Candy said.

"No."

She got up and reached out toward me, and we began to dance, moving in a small circle on the narrow balcony, with the music drifting down. With her shoes off she was considerably smaller and her head reached only to my shoulder.

"Would you care to marry me?"

She was quiet. The water on the sound was quiet. Easy swells looking green and deep rolled in quietly toward us and broke gently onto the beach.

Susan said, "I don't know."

"I was under a different impression," I said.

"So was I."

"I was under the impression that you wanted to marry me and were angry that I had not yet asked."

"That was the impression I was under too," Susan said.

"Songs unheard are sweeter far," I said.

"No, it's not that, availability makes you no less lovable. It's . . . I don't know. Isn't that amazing. I think I wanted the assurance of your asking, more than I wanted the consummated fact."

I looked at Candy again. There was nothing more to see there either. Still, I looked down at her. The rain was hard now, and dense, washing down on her upturned face. The wind was warm no longer. Candy didn't care. My clothing was soaked, my hair plastered flat against my skull. Rain running off my forehead blurred my vision. Candy's mascara had run, streaking her face. I stared down as the rain washed it away too.

"Some bodyguard," I said.

I left her there in the rain with the headlights shining on her and walked back.

The still waters began to roil slightly. The pellucid silence began to clot. I became distinct from the lake.

"Human voices wake us," I said, "and we drown."

CHAPTER 45

"What's he saying?" Linda said.

"He's still drunk from anesthesia," a nurse said.

"I want to get out of here," I said.

"How long will he babble like that?" Linda said.

"He's had a real jolt," the nurse said. "It will take a while. If you need me, ring that bell."

"How long have I been in here?" I said.

Linda patted my cheek. "Yes, honey, yes."

My right side felt as if it had been scraped raw. I put my left hand out to Linda. She smiled and took it.

"He's awake," she said.

"Alive," I said.

Linda leaned toward me, "What, love?"

"Alive," I said.

"Yes," she said. "Yes. Alive."

"Hot damn."

Linda leaned over and kissed me. "You are going to be fine," she said. "There's a policeman here."

I turned my head carefully. Frank Belson was sitting on the window ledge in his shirt sleeves, his gun butt forward on his belt, a cold cigar in his mouth.

"They won't let me smoke," he said.

"They spoil everything," I said. "How long I been here?"

I held Linda's hand as hard as I could. Which wasn't very hard.

"Three days," Linda said. "You had no pulse when they brought you in."

"They were worrying about brain death," Belson said, "but there was no way to tell."

"You're darling to wake up to, Frank."

"He's been here every day," Linda said. "He and another policeman and a man named Hawk."

"Quirk?" I said.

Belson nodded.

"Marty's been curious about the three stiffs plus you." He grinned. "Almost four."

I nodded. The nod was a mistake. It made my whole right side hurt.

"We'll talk about it later," I said.

Belson said, "Sure."

"The girl dead too?"

"Yeah. Somebody broke her neck. Hawk brought you in." Belson chewed the cold cigar butt into a better position in his mouth. "Hawk don't shed a lot of light on things."

Linda's hand was motionless in mine. Her eyes were fixed on my face. This was the part she didn't like. The part Susan knew about and didn't like.

"You okay?" I said to Linda.

She took in a deep breath and let it out and nodded.

"Susan know?" I said.

"Paul was going to call her," Linda said. "Hawk said no. He said you'd decide when you woke up."

I was slipping again. Sleep would feel a lot better than my right side. I let myself sleep and in a little while my side stopped hurting. I could feel Linda's hand in mine a long time after my side stopped hurting, well after I was otherwise asleep.

The next time I woke up Linda was gone and so was Belson. Hawk was there and Paul. As I came out of the sleep I heard Paul's voice, softly.

"No, like this, shuffle, ball, change. You see, shuffle, ball, change." I heard his feet move

266

lightly on the hospital floor. "How can a man with your heritage not be able to tap-dance."

I heard Hawk's gliding chuckle. "My ancestors busy eating missionaries, boy. We didn't have no time for no fucking shuffle ball change."

"Well, you wanted me to show you."

"That's before I knew you was going to do it better than me," Hawk said.

"Hey," I said, "Heckle and Jeckle. Don't you realize there's a wounded man in here?"

They appeared at the foot of the bed.

Paul said, "How do you feel?"

"Pretty good, I think. Where's Linda?"

"Home, asleep," Hawk said. "She about ready to fall over."

"How long have I been sleeping?" I said.

"Day and a half," Paul said. "You woke up yesterday morning."

"How bad am I?" I said to Hawk.

"This the Easter season for you, babe," Hawk said. "You was dead when we brought you in."

"I know, Belson told me."

"But you gonna make it."

I looked at Paul. He nodded. "You were in surgery for fifteen hours," he said. "You got a drain in your right side."

I nodded very carefully. "I figured that was what that was."

And then I faded out again. And woke up in daylight again with a frizz-headed doctor looking at me.

"I just want you to know," I said, "that I'm opposed to socialized medicine."

"Me too," he said. "My name is McCafferty, I did most of the work on your thoracic cavity when they brought you in here."

"Too late now, but I think my health insurance lapsed," I said.

He smiled. "We'll find a way," he said. "Do you want the details of what happened to you medically?"

"Sure."

"First, I've never seen anyone as dead as you were come back. You are one tough specimen."

"But gentle of heart," I said.

"Yes. Well, you took two bullets. Thirty-eight caliber. One went in here." He touched my right side lightly, and for the next ten minutes told me in graphic detail what had happened to my thoracic cavity as a result of being hit with two .38-caliber bullets.

"And there's nothing permanent?"

He shook his head. "As far as I can tell, there is no permanently disabling condition. In two or three months you'll be as good as you ever were."

"I was hoping for better," I said.

"Settle for what you were," he said. "It was what enabled you to survive. Tell you the truth, I didn't think you'd make it either. The black man who brought you in was the only one. He said you'd come back."

"I was a long ways away," I said. "Thank you."

McCafferty smiled. "My pleasure," he said.

I closed my eyes, and began to drift. I could feel McCafferty still there. I half opened my eyes and he was looking down at me.

"Interesting," he said half aloud. "Interesting as hell."

I closed my eyes again and drifted away.

CHAPTER 46

Linda came when she could. I was sitting up having some beef broth when she came on her lunch hour. The drain was still in my side, but most of the raw feeling was gone, and the IV apparatus was unhooked. She kissed me as hard as my condition permitted.

"Have you talked with Susan yet?" she said.

"No. She called and Paul told her I was out of town."

"Why don't you tell her?"

"Because she'd come," I said. "She'd come because she'd feel I needed her, not because she simply wanted to be with me."

"And that won't do?"

"No. When she wants to see me just because she wants to, not because I've been shot, or she might lose me, or she's afraid of something in her life, then I will want to see her."

"She will," Linda said.

"We'll see."

"She will. I would."

I held her hand.

"I don't know what will become of us if that happens," I said.

"You mean we might not be able to be lovers?"

"Maybe not," I said. "I don't know. I can't say for sure. But maybe not."

Linda began to cry. As she cried she talked.

"For crissake," she said. "She's screwing another guy, she walked out and left you, and won't even tell you where she is. She hasn't even explained why she left exactly."

"She doesn't know," I said. "Exactly."

"So how long, for crissake, will you wait for her. What does she have to do to make you give it up?"

I put my soup down, and tried to keep my breathing easy.

"There's no deadline," I said. "And no conditions."

"So the fact we love each other and might be happy together and she's banging some guy in California, or maybe several, that

271

doesn't mean anything. If she comes back, you chase right home to her?"

"I don't know," I said. "I don't know who she'll be or who I'll be, or what will come out of this. I'm saying only that I can't promise. You've known that since we started."

"And you won't give up," she said.

I shook my head. Linda put her hands over her face.

I reached out from the bed, but I couldn't reach her. Her eyes were red and her face was puffy when she lifted her head from her hands.

"What kind of a man accepts that," she said. "Allows a woman to treat him that way and keeps hanging on."

"My kind," I said. "It's why I wouldn't die. I'm going to see this through. I'm going to find out how it comes out. I love you, Linda. But I . . ." It was hard to say.

The room was quiet. Linda and I looked at each other. While the hospital went about its routine we stayed poised on this silent epicenter. Then Linda stood and bent over the bed and put her cheek against mine.

"God, you're strong," she said. "No wonder they couldn't kill you."

I stroked her hip with my left hand.

"What will become of us," she murmured

as she rubbed her cheek slowly up and down against mine.

I continued to stroke her hip. "I don't know," I said. "The past is painful, maybe even fraudulent, the future is uncertain, maybe scary. What we have is a continuing present, honey. I think we should do what we can with that."

She shook her head against me. "I don't think so," she said.

CHAPTER 47

It was a big morning for me. I didn't drink any coffee. A doctor and two nurses came in and removed the drain from my side. And an hour later Rita Fiori came in to visit me. And she wore a green tailored suit with a frilly white collar spilling out at the throat.

"Mind if I smoke," she said.

"Not at all," I said. "Want to hear about how I quit in 1968 and haven't had a puff since and don't miss it?"

"Only if you promise to explain in great and graphic detail to me how bad it is for my health and how my lungs must look. I always enjoy that."

She took some Tareyton 100's out of her

purse and stuck one into her mouth and lit it with a Cricket lighter and took a big drag and blew it out away from me.

"For crissake," she said, "I don't even enjoy it." She sat, crossed her legs, and put her cigarette back into her mouth while she rummaged in her purse. She was wearing white stockings. It was the current look and I hoped it would pass quickly. Her shoes had three-inch heels.

"We've been trying to figure out what happened with Paultz and Winston and the Spellman kid."

"Sherry," I said.

"Yeah." Rita took another drag and looked down at her notebook. I looked at her legs. "We had a bunch of questions and no answers so we checked back and we pieced together and sometimes we guessed. But the best we can get looks a little like this. Winston was the brains of the thing. How he and Paultz got together we don't know. There aren't many of them around to tell us." Rita looked at me directly.

I nodded. "Maybe there's some truth to the story he told me," I said.

"Maybe. Anyway, they did get together and it was a natural match. Winston had missions in Turkey, in Southeast Asia, places where they can raise opium poppies. He had missionaries who could mule the raw heroin into here. Paultz had a market and he had a system for cutting and packaging and getting it into retail hands."

"Was Winston doing this from the beginning?" I said.

"I don't think so," Rita said. She recrossed her legs and showed me some thigh in the process. I was pleased. "He probably started it because of religious belief and desire for power and position, and the chance to manipulate people." She shrugged. "You know. And then it came along. We don't know how, either. Maybe a local mission head started dealing small and Winston found out and saw the potential. Maybe it was Paultz's idea." She shook her head and shrugged again.

"Anyway," she said, "Winston would sell the heroin to Paultz and then lend money back to Paultz's construction company at a little below market rates. It gave the church a nice clean income—earnings from loans to a large construction firm. It gave Paultz a way to account for his income—loans to his construction company from an established church."

"A kind of double wash," I said.

"Yep," Rita said, "reciprocal laundering. There's still more to that part and some of it is quite fancy. The accountants will be able to givo you some of the more elegant nuances later. But that's the gross outline of it."

"Gross outlines are about all I can handle," I said. "Elegant nuances would be beyond me."

"Watching you charge around on this one, I'm inclined to believe you," Rita said.

"I was distracted," I said.

Rita nodded. Her cigarette was out and she got another from the pack and lit it. "That's what Quirk told me." She made a dismissive wiggle with the hand holding the cigarette. "Be that as it may. You had it backwards when you brought Winston into that meeting. And we bought it. We all thought Paultz was running Winston when in fact Winston was running Paultz."

"And when I started to find the connection between them," I said, "he figured a way to dump Paultz and get out from under and keep the heroin business in exchange for backing away from the church and maybe a short jail term."

"Yes, as long as he could kill Paultz before Paultz told his side. We figure Paultz went for the trust deal to stall until he found out what Winston was up to."

"At which point he'd have killed Winston," I said.

Rita smiled. "Yes. It was pretty much a two-man swindle. Each was the only one that could connect the other one."

"Which brings us to Sherry," I said.

"Dear little Sherry," Rita said. "Twenty years old, the soul of piety and love. She jerked you clowns around like trout."

"It's not that simple," I said.

"Why isn't it," Rita said.

"Because it isn't. Hell, nothing is, not really. She killed Paultz. Winston asked her to and she did and by that point it probably didn't bother her. But she wasn't just a girl who'd shoot someone. She loved Winston, I think. And she loved Tommy Banks."

"Wouldn't it be pretty to think so," Rita said.

"Christ, a literate prosecutor," I said.

"Literate and sexy," she said.

"They're all sexy," I said. "It's the literate that makes you special."

"She did it all for love?" Rita said.

"No, I don't know if she even knew what she did it all for. But she was a kid looking for a place. She tried dancing and religion. She tried loving Tommy and Winston. Paul says she wrote poetry. She wanted to be something that mattered or that was exciting or that wasn't ordinary. Under different circumstances she'd be taking courses at the Adult

Ed Center in Cambridge, and working on a play."

Rita sucked in the corners of her mouth and shook her head.

"Or she might have gone to law school," I said. "And when the money and the power of the dope deal came along it hooked her. She wouldn't give it up and she wouldn't stop being powerful and rich and she would do anything not to go back to writing poetry and trying to dance and thinking about religion and so she shot Paultz and then when Winston wouldn't tell the truth even to save her she turned on him and finally on me. I was all that was left to keep her from her place."

"Maybe," Rita said. "Or maybe she was a conniving little bitch that bamboozled all of you."

"She'd never have spent as much time with Tommy as she did. She'd have latched on to Winston and stayed. But she didn't, she vacillated. She came back to Tommy, then went back to Winston, why would she try and be with Tommy if she was simply after money and power?"

"And Paultz didn't know anything about her?"

"No reason he should," I said. "And a lot of reason, once Winston was backing away from the church, that he shouldn't. Maybe Winston always knew he might need a straw. Maybe he kept her relationship with him secret so he could use her when he needed her."

"How about Banks," Rita said. "What made him suspicious all of a sudden?"

"Jealousy. He may have known her better than he could admit. He may have always known she was bitchier than she acted. But until he lost her and couldn't get her back, he didn't care. I think he started following her simply for a way to keep in contact. Knowledge is power, you know, and if he could spy her out and follow her around and know what she was doing . . . It was like he still had some control. I don't think he was suspicious about the heroin deal. I think he just stumbled on it and decided to use it as a way to get her back. It's all he ever really wanted. To have her and control her and, you know, own her."

"Ain't love grand," Rita said.

"So what happens to the Bullies?"

"Norfolk County doesn't care," Rita said. "Unless they get back in the skag business again. They got a nice trust fund, I understand, and doubtless a new and charismatic leader will emerge to help them spend it."

"Ah, Rita, so young, so cynical," I said.

"But literate," she said. "And sexy."

"Perhaps," I said, "when I get out of here I

should buy you a drink and discuss books with you."

"Good thought," she said. "Keep in mind, too, when you get out of here, that Joe Broz will not be among your boosters. He wanted Winston's source and he got nothing. It will annoy him."

"A day is not wasted if you've annoyed Joe Broz," I said.

"Well, be a little careful," she said. "At least until we've had our drink."

"And had a literate discussion," I said.

"Literate and sexy," she said.

"Yes."

CHAPTER 48

It was nearly ten at night in Boston when I called Susan in San Francisco.

"How are you," she said. Her voice still small with pain. "Paul said you were out of town."

"I'm good," I said. "How are you?"

"I'm . . . I'm not good," she said. "I'm in therapy."

"That should help," I said. "In a while at least."

"Yes," she said. The pause seemed longer on the open phone line. "I . . . how bad has it been about my friend?" she said.

"Worst thing that ever happened to me," I said.

"How do you stand it?"

"Tough kid," I said. "Always been a tough kid."

Again the silence stretching across the darkening land.

"He's gone," Susan said.

It was like not drowning. I took a breath. *Steady*.

"He's gone back to his wife," she said.

"He's got a wife?"

"Yes." Susan's voice was tiny.

"Jesus Christ," I said.

And then her voice wasn't small. "I will not leave you," she said.

"In a manner of speaking."

I could hear the smile in her voice. "In a manner of speaking."

"He wanted to move in?" I said.

"He wanted to divorce his wife and marry me."

"And you wouldn't."

Again the strength. "I will not leave you," she said.

"Nor I you," I said.

"Do you suppose you could get away for a little while?" Susan said.

"In two weeks I can get away for as long as I want to."

"Would you come to San Francisco and visit me?"

"Yes."

"In two weeks?"

"Yes."

"It makes me feel less scared," Susan said.

"Me too," I said. "It makes me want to sing 'I Left My Heart in San Francisco.' "

"It does?"

"Yeah," I said. "Want to hear me sing a couple choruses in perfect imitation of Tony Bennett?"

"No," Susan said, "not ever." And she laughed. And I laughed. And the two of us sat alone and far, and laughed carefully together at the verge of different oceans.

(#1. 2-2-86)